D0722487

The Ghost of
Apache Creek

**Center Point
Large Print**

Also by Joseph A. West and available from Center Point Large Print:

The Stranger of Abilene
The Burning Range
The Last Manhunt

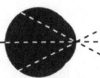

This Large Print Book carries the Seal of Approval of N.A.V.H.

Ralph Compton

The Ghost of Apache Creek

A Ralph Compton Novel

JOSEPH A. WEST

CENTER POINT LARGE PRINT
THORNDIKE, MAINE

This Center Point Large Print edition is published
in the year 2012 by arrangement with NAL Signet,
a member of Penguin Group (USA) Inc.

Copyright © The Estate of Ralph Compton, 2011

All rights reserved.

This is a work of fiction. Names, characters, places, and
incidents either are the product of the author's imagination
or are used fictitiously, and any resemblance to actual
persons, living or dead, business establishments, events, or
locales is entirely coincidental.

The text of this Large Print edition is unabridged.
In other aspects, this book may
vary from the original edition.
Printed in the United States of America
on permanent paper.
Set in 16-point Times New Roman type.

ISBN: 978-1-61173-403-4

Library of Congress Cataloging-in-Publication Data

Compton, Ralph.
The ghost of Apache creek : a Ralph Compton novel / Joseph A. West
and Ralph Compton.
p. cm. — (Center point large print edition)
ISBN 978-1-61173-403-4 (library binding : alk. paper)
1. Large type books. I. West, Joseph A. II. Title.
PS3553.O48435G56 2012
813′.54—dc23

2012003142

The Immortal Cowboy

This is respectfully dedicated to the "American Cowboy." His was the saga sparked by the turmoil that followed the Civil War, and the passing of more than a century has by no means diminished the flame.

True, the old days and the old ways are but treasured memories, and the old trails have grown dim with the ravages of time, but the spirit of the cowboy lives on.

In my travels—to Texas, Oklahoma, Kansas, Nebraska, Colorado, Wyoming, New Mexico, and Arizona—I always find something that reminds me of the Old West. While I am walking these plains and mountains for the first time, there is this feeling that a part of me is eternal, that I have known these old trails before. I believe it is the undying spirit of the frontier calling me, through the mind's eye, to step back into time. What is the appeal of the Old West of the American frontier?

It has been epitomized by some as the dark and bloody period in American history. Its heroes—

Crockett, Bowie, Hickok, Earp—have been reviled and criticized. Yet the Old West lives on, larger than life.

It has become a symbol of freedom, when there was always another mountain to climb and another river to cross; when a dispute between two men was settled not with expensive lawyers, but with fists, knives, or guns. Barbaric? Maybe. But some things never change. When the cowboy rode into the pages of American history, he left behind a legacy that lives within the hearts of us all.

—Ralph Compton

Chapter 1

Dry lightning shimmered silver on the warped timbers of the town, imparting a fleeting beauty. A hard wind broke in waves over the Mogollon Rim to the south, crested, and then rampaged north toward the peaks and mesas of the White Mountains, picking up ragged veils of sand as it went.

The wind venomously hurled the sand against the ghost town of Requiem as though trying to wake the place from its deep slumber. Stinging grit cartwheeled along Main Street and rattled against the cracked glass of store windows, threatening to break them further. Rusty-hinged doors squealed and slammed in the tempest, and the wind shrieked like a virgin saint forced to take partners for the Devil's barn dance.

A tall man walked through this maelstrom of wind, sand, and darkness, his head bent, seemingly oblivious to his surroundings. His boots thudded on the boardwalk, the chime of his spurs faint in the storm's roar. He stepped along slowly, shoulders hunched, long hair tumbling down his ragged back.

The man could have been a sleepwalker, lost in a nightmare, or a wandering drifter seeking shelter from the storm. But Marshal Sam Pace was neither of those things. He was aware. Alert. Ready. And he was listening. The dead were talking. . . . He heard their thin whispers in the wind.

He stopped and lifted his head, his eyes bright.

"Is that you?" he said, raising his voice to a shout. "John Andres, is that you calling to me?"

He listened into the night, hard-driven sand hissing over him.

Pace opened the twisted door of Big John's Bakery and Pie Shop and stepped inside; the storm, frustrated for the moment, let him go.

"John?" Pace said. "Why did you call out to me?"

The bakery was angled in deep shadow. Its shelves were empty, gray with cobwebs, and the place smelled of pack rats and dry rot.

"Where the hell are you, John?" Pace said. "Martha, are you there?"

Something rustled in a corner. The wind pounded at the store window, demanding entry. The door grated on its hinges.

But the pie shop was a tomb, dark, empty, without human life.

Sudden realization spiked in Pace, startling him.

There was no one here. Not a soul.

Big John, big laughing John Andres, who had won a medal at Gettysburg and another at Cold Harbor, was dead of the cholera these past three years. He'd buried Martha himself, a plump, rosy-cheeked woman who'd baked the best apple pie in the county and made biscuits so light they almost floated. John and Martha had moldered long in the ground and nothing about them would look human any longer.

Still, he tried again. "John? Martha? Are you there?"

A hollow silence mocked him. Outside, the wind raved and ranted, impatient for his return.

Pace stumbled to the door and once again stepped into uproar.

But wait. He was in no rush to walk again. It was time for thought.

He sheltered in a store doorway, feeling crafty, because he knew there was much mischief afoot. Chin in hand, he pondered the wind. *Aha,* now he knew. It came from the northwest.

"Do you know what that means, Sam?" he said aloud.

He answered his own question, the habit of a man who has spent too much time alone.

"Sure do, Sam. It means you'll only be insane until the wind shifts."

Pace nodded and smiled. He was happy that he'd gotten to the truth of the thing.

Earlier in the day, the wind had blown from the south, and he'd been perfectly sane. But within the last hour it had shifted. When it blew from the south again, he'd be his old rational self.

William Shakespeare said he would, and ol' Will knew about such things, him being a famous playwright an' all.

"I am but mad north-north west. When the wind is southerly I know a hawk from a handsaw."

For some reason, Pace had always remembered that quote since he'd heard an actor say it at a theater in Deadwood, and it tickled him. He said it aloud. Then once again.

But another thought silenced him.

"Sam," he said aloud, his face puzzled, "when the wind was from the south, how come you were still crazy as a loon?"

Pace shook his shaggy head.

"Sam doesn't know," he said. He thought about it. "I reckon ol' Will Shakespeare has some explaining to do. That's what I think."

The marshal stumbled into the street, and again got pummeled by wind and hammered by stinging sand.

"Will Shakespeare!" he yelled, throwing his arms wide, his head back. "You know nothing! You don't know shit!" He laughed, an empty noise without humor. "Damn you, when the wind was from the south I was still stark, raving mad and I didn't know a hawk from a handsaw!"

Pace looked beyond the edge of town, his eyes cunning again as they searched the darkness.

Now he had a plan, a good plan.

The graveyard was out there, hidden in the gloom.

"Sam," he said, "the best thing you can do now is to talk to Jane and the baby. You can tell them about the south wind and how Shakespeare doesn't know nothin'."

Pace nodded. Yes, he'd do that. Jane would understand his madness and give him comfort.

The cemetery had been laid out just two hundred yards beyond the town limits. Because of flooding considerations, it lay atop a shallow rise at the base of a bare rock ridge shaped like the bow of a steamship.

Once the place had been a sun-dappled, grassy spot, but now it was overrun with brush and cactus, and the site of the mass grave left a rectangular scar that would last for years.

Pace had walked to the cemetery every day for the past three years and knew the way, his feet feeling out the path in inky, sand-torn darkness. The mass grave had no marker, but Pace found it easily, a tall wild oak guiding him to the spot. He knew the place well, and why not? He'd buried eighty-three people here, him and big John Andres, among them Pace's own wife and child, taken by the cholera. At the end, the last bodies he'd rolled into the pit had been those of John and his wife, Martha.

Before then, the town had been known as

11

Apache Creek, but when folks started dying, the mayor issued a decree that from henceforth it would bear the name Requiem.

No one had disagreed with him—at least, none of those who were still alive.

Pace's hat had blown away in the storm, but he clasped his hands in front of him, bowed his head, and waited as always for Jane to talk first. The wind roughed up the oak and Pace heard the *tick-tick-tick* of blown sand hitting the tree's leaves and trunk. He stood stock-still for an hour, waiting with a madman's rigid patience for Jane to talk to him. But she didn't whisper to him, to tell him to be faithful and brave. Not this night.

And all the while, Pace turned slowly into a pillar of sand.

His matted hair and long beard were stiff and yellow, the rags he wore gritty, the color of earth. His eyes were rimmed with red, and dirt gathered at the corners of his mouth.

Filthy, smelly, overgrown with hair—this night, Sam Pace looked more animal than human. His untrimmed nails curved like talons. Those and his fiery gaze gave him the appearance of a dangerous scavenger come to raid the graves of the dead.

Only one thing about Marshal Sam Pace was clean—the oiled blue Colt shoved into the pocket of his ragged pants.

The habits of a lifetime die hard, and Pace had lived long with the Colt and knew its ways. He lavished care on the big revolver, but none on himself. Such was the manner of the gunfighting lawman, a reverence for the tool of his trade that not even madness could alter.

Finally Pace stirred. He talked to Jane for a while, and asked her to kiss the baby for him.

"On her cheeks," he said. "I always loved to kiss her chubby little cheeks."

Then he turned and walked back toward town.

Suddenly he stopped in his tracks. He knew why Jane said nothing to him—she was afraid to make a sound.

It was the same reason the people who'd fled the cholera had not yet returned to Requiem.

Outlaws! Damn them!

Pace stood in the middle of the street, his Colt in his hand. He couldn't see the bad men, not yet, but they were here all right, lurking in the shadows, ready to rob the bank and hoorah the town.

Marshal Sam Pace's town.

His face took on a determined look as he raised his gun to waist level, his thumb on the hammer. He'd show them. Teach them that Sam Pace was no bargain.

"I'm ready for you skunks," he yelled. "Come the hell out and take your medicine like men."

There! Slinking into the alley by the Oxford Hat Shoppe. The outlaw was crouched, ready to take aim at him.

Pace thumbed off a shot and then ran for the alley. He was just in time to see the man, a fleeting shadow crawling on his hands and knees, disappear around a corner.

There was a splash of blood in the sand, then a scarlet trail leading toward the rear into the alley. Well, that fatherless son of a bitch wouldn't be back for another dose of Marshal Sam Pace anytime soon.

Pace angled across the street to the bank, wind and sand tearing at him. His face set and hard, his eyes reached into the darkness.

He saw movement—another damned outlaw crawling like a dog on all fours!—and fired. He was rewarded by the man's yelp of pain and he fired again. This time the outlaw dropped and sprawled on the boardwalk.

"Got you," Pace said. "That'll teach you that you can't rob banks and scare folks in my town."

He thumbed back the hammer of his Colt and walked toward the dead man. He stepped onto the boardwalk, then stumbled as his boot crashed through a rotted timber. Pace fell to his left and his head struck something hard. Lightning flashed inside his skull, followed by blackness. He heard the fading sound of the roaring night . . . then nothing at all.

Chapter 2

"Who the hell are you?"

Pace opened his eyes, squinting against the glare of the harsh morning sun. Inches from his face were the front legs of a horse, a steeldust with two white socks.

"I'll ask you again," the man's voice said. "There won't be a third time." A pause, then: "Who the hell are you?"

Pace struggled to his feet and held on to a post for support. His head throbbed and the sunlight spiked viciously at his eyes. He tried to speak, but his voice was a dry croak.

Five men sat their horses, studying him. The man who had spoken—big, blond, and flashily handsome—was smiling. But it was a smile of contempt, not humor.

Pace put his fingers to the back of his head and they came away bloody.

"Did one of you rannies buffalo me?" he said.

"Hell no," the blond man said. "Near as I can tell you got drunk, fell down, and hit your damn fool head."

He looked beyond Pace to the bank porch. "You shoot that coyote, did ye?"

15

Pace turned and saw what the big man had seen. "I reckon so."

"You mean you don't know?"

"I see things sometimes. I guess I mistook him for an outlaw, a bank robber."

"There are no banks to rob in a ghost town, mister."

"No. I reckon not," Pace said.

The man on the steeldust grinned. "God, you're a sight."

"And he stinks," another man said.

"What are you doing here?" the blond man asked.

Pace grabbed the bottom of his left sleeve between fingers and palm and rubbed sand off the star on his chest. "I'm marshal of this town."

The big man looked around him, and then his men joined in his laughter. His horse tossed its head, the bit chiming.

"Maybe you haven't noticed . . . Marshal, but there's nobody here, 'cept you," he said.

"They'll be back. One day the people will come back to Requiem." He pointed to the far end of town. "They'll come off the trail yonder and head into town and their wagons will stretch for a mile and the kids will be running beside them. Then they'll change the name back to what it once was, Apache Creek. That's what they'll do all right."

"That's what you think, huh?" the big man said.

"That's what I know," Pace said.

"And this place is now called Requiem?"

"Yes. Just that."

"Good. It's an apt name for a dead town."

The big man shifted position in the saddle. "My name's Beau Harcourt." He waved a hand. "All of this is my range, and you're on it. So what do we do about that?"

Pace saw his Colt lying on the ground several feet away, a fact that brought him no comfort.

"Mr. Harcourt, this is my town. You may own the range around it, but you don't own Requiem."

"I've got a different opinion on that. What happened here anyhow?"

"Three years ago we got took by the cholera. Four score citizens and more now lie in the graveyard. The rest lit out. But they'll be back and find their lawman waiting for them."

"You?"

"Me."

That last brought guffaws from Harcourt's hard-faced riders.

Talking above the laughter, the big man said, "You cut your hair, shaved, or bathed in them three years . . . Marshal?"

"Maybe. But not that I recall. Sometimes I get loco, tetched in the head, and then I don't remember to do things. I don't remember any-thing, except the cholera. But sometimes I can tell a hawk from a handsaw, when the wind is right."

17

"Hell, what do you eat? Lizards?"

"When the store owners pulled out, they left stuff behind. I eat from cans. I eat peaches and beans and meat sometimes."

Harcourt grinned. "No matter, a man should remember to take a bath." He tilted his head to the side and his grin faded to a smile. "You got a horse?"

"Yes, at the livery."

"Then saddle up and get out of here while you still can."

"I can't do that."

"Because all them dead people will come back and expect to find you here?"

"No, the folks who left will come back."

"How do you know?"

"I just know."

"Man, you're even crazier than I thought you were. What's your name, wild man?"

"Do you care?"

"No. But I still want to hear it."

"Sam Pace."

A tall rider wearing a fringed buckskin jacket stiffened in the saddle and said, "Well, I'll be."

"Something bothering you, Heap?" Harcourt said.

The man called Heap ignored the question and said, "Were you the Sam Pace out of Cochise County?"

"There and other places," Pace said.

Heap nodded, then answered the question on Harcourt's face. "Gunfighter. Or he was. He wore a Ranger's star when he killed Dixie Tavern back in seventy-five, and Dixie was fast on the draw."

"He sure don't look like much now."

"No, he don't, boss. That's fer sure."

Heap watched absently as Harcourt shook out his rope.

Finally, as though he'd just fitted words to a thought, he said, "Back in the day, Pace was hell on wheels with a gun; killed his share. Even a crazy man don't lose that."

Harcourt frowned at Pace. "Is that right? You good with a gun?"

"I manage," Pace said.

Harcourt sat back in the saddle, the rope swinging idly in his right hand.

"For some reason you worry me," he said, "and I don't like being worried."

The rope snaked out and the loop dropped neatly over Pace's shoulders, then dropped to his ankles.

"But all that changes right now," Harcourt said. "Time to read to you from the book."

He kicked the steeldust into a gallop.

Pace was yanked off his feet and sent tumbling into the dirt. His body spun as Harcourt let rip with a rebel yell and dragged him into the street.

Pace's world narrowed to the billowing cloud

of yellow dust that enveloped him and the pain that scraped mercilessly at his belly, back, and thighs. He opened his mouth and tried to roar his outrage and anger. But his mouth filled with sand and he could only croak. His throat clogged and he vomited green bile on himself.

Somewhere he heard men laugh.

Chapter 3

Sam Pace lost count of how many times Harcourt dragged him up and down the street behind his running horse. A lot. That much he knew. Finally, after what seemed an eternity, Pace's cartwheeling body came to a stop and he felt the pressure of the rope around his ankles ease.

Harcourt's voice came from a long way off, from somewhere beyond the settling dust cloud.

"Boys," the big rancher said, "Marshal Pace will take his bath now. And a shave and a haircut."

Four of Harcourt's grinning riders, hooting and hollering, scrambled off their horses and grabbed Pace, dragging him to his feet.

"Fill a horse trough," one of the men said. He nodded. "Over there, outside the saloon."

The trough was of zinc-lined wood, green with algae and slime. A couple of Harcourt's riders took turns to shuttle a bucket from the well, stopping only when the water was an inch from the top.

Pace slowly understood what was about to happen to him. He glanced across the street to where his Colt lay, half buried in sand. He tried to stagger toward the gun. He was abraded bloody from head to toe, the front of his left thigh gouged by a broken whiskey bottle Harcourt had gone out of his way to gallop over.

Pace struck out at a man trying to drag him to the trough. His fist connected solidly with the man's chin and the cowboy went down like a felled ox.

Pace paid dearly for that.

He was wrestled to the ground and the boots went in, thudding into his ribs and face. He tried to cover up, but the kicks found their target every time, thumping into his body, beating like the sound of a muffled drum.

"Enough. I don't want the crazy nut dead."

Harcourt's voice.

Pace was hauled to his feet. Through swollen, half-shut eyes, he saw the rancher sit his horse, grinning.

Almost unconscious from the beating he'd taken, his head reeling, Pace had enough awareness to realize that he wanted to kill Beau Harcourt real bad.

"Mr. Pace's bath now, if you please," Harcourt said.

"Still want us to give him a shave an' a haircut, boss?" a man asked.

"Of course. Can't you see? It's what the gentleman needs."

Pace was stripped of his filthy rags and tossed into the horse trough. Somebody found a mostly bald scrubbing brush, but there were bristles enough left to shred the already sand-scoured skin of Pace's belly and back. Pace growled and roared and fought, striking out at his tormentors, but he was weak from loss of blood and the pounding Harcourt's riders were still dishing out with their fists and the heavy wooden brush.

After a few minutes, there was blood in the water of the trough and fury in Pace's eyes, the black, all-consuming anger of a crazy man.

The cowboys laughed and joshed each other, enjoying the sport. Then they took out their knives. They were Barlow folders for the most part. Nevertheless, their carbon steel blades were honed sharp and their owners wielded them with enthusiasm. The punchers started on Pace's hair, sawing at thick clumps they yanked upward and gathered in their fists. Skeletal fingers of blood trickled from Pace's head as ragged bunches of hair joined the crimson gore in the trough, making a vile stew of the man's misery. The keen blades dug deep as they scraped along Pace's cheeks and chin, shaving off skin along with beard. Now his face bled and crimson drops dripped off his chin.

Pace made a lunge for a man's knife, but the puncher hit him with a vicious left and his eye swelled closed.

He heard Harcourt's voice.

"How's he looking, boys?"

"Real purty," a man said.

"Well, he's had enough, I reckon," Harcourt said. "Get him out of there."

Finally it was over. Dragging him, dripping wet, from the trough, the Harcourt riders threw Pace in front of their boss's steeldust.

"Haul him to his feet," the rancher said.

Harcourt stared at Pace for a long time. Then he said, "Well, Marshal Pace, you don't worry me any longer, you being so nicely bathed and groomed an' all."

Men laughed and Harcourt said, "You got a day to rest up, a day to get your shit together, and a day to contemplate the errors of your ways. After that, I don't want to see you in this town any-more."

Harcourt's eyes swept over Pace. The man was now diminished, a bleeding, dripping wreck who was a threat to nobody, and the rancher lost interest in him.

"Do you understand?" he said.

Pace's tongue was thick in his cracked and bloody mouth, but he managed.

"You go to hell," he said.

Beau Harcourt shook his head. "Aw, the heck

with it," he said, resignation and contempt battling for elbow room in his voice.

He rode up on Pace, freed his right foot from the stirrup, and kicked the bloody man hard in the face. Pace dropped and lay still.

"You've got a big mouth, mister," Harcourt said. "Time you kept it shut."

"Hey, boss, lookee."

One of Harcourt's riders had led a tall blue roan Appaloosa from the livery stable.

"Ain't he a beauty?" the puncher said. "He's a two-hundred-dollar hoss any day of the week."

Harcourt acknowledged that with a nod, then said, "Seems like Marshal Pace wasn't so crazy he forgot to take care of his horse."

"What will I do with him?"

"The hoss? Take him with us, of course."

The rider nodded in the direction of Pace's sprawled body. "What about him?"

"If he recovers, he can walk," Harcourt said. He pointed south. "Old Mexico is only three hundred miles thataway, give or take."

Chapter 4

Sam Pace opened his eyes and looked into a gathering dusk.

Harcourt and his men were gone and he was alone in the street. Shadows angled in the alleys and a solemn hush lay over the town. Only the *thud-thud-thud* of an opening and shutting door was loud, like a booted man walking in a cathedral.

Pace tried to get to his feet, failed, and gratefully sank to his belly again. The wind felt cool against his cheek and somehow the growing darkness was soothing, easing away his pain.

His gun was about six feet away, only part of the handle sticking up from the sand. He crawled toward the Colt, leaving a bloody slug-trail behind him.

After shaking grit from the revolver, Pace tried to rise again. This time he succeeded, swaying on his feet, his world rocking around him as though he were caught in a mighty earthshake. He laid the Colt on the boardwalk, taken by an idea that might help soothe his hurt.

Naked, shivering from cold brought on by the beating he'd taken and loss of blood, Pace staggered in the direction of the creek that ran deep and clear to the east of town. The hundred-yard journey took him an hour. He fell constantly as he passed in and out of consciousness. Each time he eventually struggled to his feet and stumbled forward a yard or so, only to fall again. A groan escaped his lips every time he slammed into the dirt.

The creek was hidden by stretching shadows, but Pace heard it bubble over its sand and pebble bottom, and a soaring cottonwood marked the bank. Slowly, painfully, on all fours, he crawled over uneven ground and rested when he reached the tree. Coyotes called in the distance, and the night birds pecked at the first stars. The wind stirred the cottonwood branches and bent the nearby willows to its will.

Pace reached the bank and let himself roll into the water. The coolness of the creek, born of a mountain, came as a shock. But Pace delighted in its tumbling waters as they numbed his pain and washed blood from his head and body.

After a while he lay on his back and watched the rising moon. It beamed at Pace, as though glad to see him again, then drew a veil of cloud across its face.

After an hour, Pace struggled to his feet and the creek rushed swiftly between his knees, threatening to unbalance him. He crawled to the bank and threw himself down on a patch of grass, breathing hard. His eyes reached into the night, in the direction of Requiem, and his mouth tightened against his teeth.

How the hell was he going to make it back?

The moon was high in the sky when Pace finally reached the boardwalk outside his office. He rested, sitting in the dirt, his bent elbow on the warped timbers, each breath heaving hard and fast. He tilted back his head and yelled into the night. "Bastards!"

He felt the Colt's hammer grit against the frame as he thumbed off a shot, then another. Smoke drifting around his naked body, he called out again, his voice hoarse into the heedless dark.

"A crazy man! Damn you all, you drug a crazy man!"

Pace pushed up on the boardwalk and got to his feet. He triggered the Colt again, but the hammer clicked on a spent round.

"Bastards!"

The naked man climbed onto the boardwalk and roared obscenities into the night, his mind shadowed with dark places where gibbering phantoms dwelled, his boon companions.

Pace stumbled into his office. His way illuminated by blades of moonlight, he slumped behind his desk. He opened a drawer, removed one of his dwindling supply of matches, and lit the candle on the desktop.

For a moment the room flared with light, then dimmed to a dull yellow shimmer that made the darkness dance and gleam like tarnished silver among the cobwebs in the corners where the silent spiders lived. A scrap of mirror hung on the wall, thick with dust and fly specks. Pace rose, wiped it off with the heel of his hand, and brought the candle close. He stared into the mirror and into the burning eyes of a madman.

The knives of Harcourt's riders had scraped part of his head into stubble, but long scalp locks still hung from several places and damp strands of hair spilled over his shoulders. His beard had received the same treatment, some areas shaved to the skin, other patches still intact, falling over his naked chest.

The candlelight, though less cruel than the glare of day, still revealed to Sam Pace what he'd become: a poor, insane creature who had surely been doomed from the moment of his birth.

He turned away from the mirror and sat at his desk again, settling the candle in front of him.

Slowly, laboriously, he cleaned and oiled his Colt. From a box of .45 shells in a drawer in his desk, he loaded five rounds and lowered the hammer on an empty chamber, the habit of a lifetime that required no thought. Years before, he'd had the Colt's action tuned by an El Paso gunsmith. It took only two pounds of pressure on the trigger to trip the hammer. And that was nothing, really. Nothing at all.

Pace cocked the revolver, its triple-click loud in the quiet. He shoved the muzzle against his temple.

All men live. Not all deserve to.

Pace put himself in that last category. What the world didn't need was another crazy man.

Chapter 5

"Boss!"

Beau Harcourt opened the tent flap and stepped outside into moonlight. "What is it, Ben?"

"Deacon Santee ain't comin' in, boss. At least not tomorrow, he ain't."

Harcourt's handsome face flashed his anger. "Why the hell not?"

"He's gettin' hitched, boss," the cowboy said. "Says the lady will be his seventh bride an' that's a lucky number. He says he's plannin' a big soiree after the . . . what did he call it? Oh yeah, the nuptials."

"Why the hell don't he bed them ladies of his and let it go at that? Why does he always have to marry them?"

"Don't know, boss," the man called Ben said. He was a tall, loose-limbed puncher with the face of a kicked hound dog. "But the deacon says he won't live with a woman without benefit of clergy, whatever that means."

"Clergy my ass."

Harcourt fished around for more words to express his frustration with Santee, but finally settled on "You see the herd?"

"As much as I could in the dark. Counts out to

a thousand head all right. I'm certain of that. He's rounded up a bunch of scrubs, though."

"Damn it, a man with a rustled herd and the Rangers right on his ass stops to get hitched. I can't figure it."

"Me neither," Ben said.

Harcourt glared at the man as though he wanted to haul off and punch him.

Ben caught the look and tried to deflect Harcourt's anger. He said, "The deacon ain't a man to be hurried, and you can't push him too hard neither. He's got a hair temper an' hair triggers on his guns."

The big rancher recognized the logic in that and let his irritation go. Hell, it wasn't Ben Trivet's fault that Santee was a stupid son of a bitch.

"There's bacon and beans in the pot an' fresh coffee," Harcourt said. "Eat, then saddle up another pony. I'm sending you out again tonight."

"He ain't gonna listen to me, boss. No more'n he done the first time."

"I know. But this time you'll be carrying a note. From me."

Trivet nodded. "Anything you say, boss. Maybe a note will make the difference—but the deacon ain't about to give up his nuptials."

As the puncher walked away, Harcourt called after him: "Heap Leggett is standing by the fire. Send him over here, will ya?"

Trivet waved a hand in acknowledgment.

• • •

"What's the problem, Beau?" Leggett said. He took a guess. "Trouble with the deacon?"

Harcourt held open the tent flap. "We'll talk inside."

Leggett sat on the cot and Harcourt took his place behind a portable field desk. He reached under the desk, found a bottle and two glasses, and poured whiskey for both of them.

The rancher studied his foreman over the rim of his glass until Leggett began to shift uncomfortably, then said, "The deacon won't be here tomorrow."

"Why not?"

"He's getting married."

Leggett smiled. "Who's gonna do the marrying? Himself?"

Harcourt shrugged. "Probably one of his crazy sons. All four of them are reverends, or so they say."

"He bring the herd?"

"A thousand head, according to Trivet. He says they're mostly scrubs."

"Trivet is an idiot."

"I know, but he knows cattle and does what he's told. Above all he's expendable."

"Beau, we got three days to push the herd to Silver Creek at the Rio Puerco," Leggett said. "It's a ways and the army won't wait. They'll buy their beef from some other outfit."

"Tell me something I don't already know," Harcourt said. He thought for a few moments. "But they'll wait a day, maybe two, if they need the beef bad enough."

"I reckon they need it bad enough," Heap Leggett said. "I hear the Apaches are starving and the young bucks are making war talk."

He was almost as tall as Harcourt, and just as handsome, as though both men had been cut from the same cloth.

Leggett had first gone up the trail to Kansas when he was fourteen. Later he'd been a Wells Fargo train guard, a town marshal, and then had graduated to hired killer.

For a three-month spell, two years before, he'd married and opened a restaurant, but it didn't work out and his wife left him.

But the catering business taught Leggett one thing—honest work was for losers.

Now, as Beau Harcourt's *segundo*, he made gun wages for very little effort and that suited him just fine. He'd killed seven men, and nary a one of them kept him awake o' nights.

Harcourt was talking again, his eye sockets and cheeks shadowed by the orange glow of the oil lamp.

"I'm sending Trivet out again, this time with a note from me to the deacon. I want that herd here. Like you say, if we don't deliver beef to the army on time, they'll buy it elsewhere."

"Suppose he still won't come?"

"Then we'll take it from him."

"Boss, Deacon Santee ain't a bargain, and neither are them crazy sons of his."

Harcourt smiled. "I know, Heap. That's why I hired you. It's time you started earning your wages."

The rancher pulled a sheet of paper toward him and began to write with a stub of pencil. He looked up from the paper.

"You afraid of the deacon, Heap?" he said, smiling.

"I'm afraid of no man."

"Can you take him?"

"Any day of the week, I can take him."

"He's fast on the draw-and-shoot, they say."

"I'm faster."

Harcourt nodded, readily accepting Leggett's word.

"Tomorrow morning ride over to that ghost town—what the hell is it called?"

"Requiem."

"Yeah, that's it. Make sure the wild man has moved on."

"Sure thing, boss. And if he's still there?"

"Kill him. I gave him his chance."

Harcourt handed the note he'd written to Ben Trivet, who had come back to the tent after finishing his dinner.

"Can you read?" he said.

The puncher nodded. "Some."

"Then read it."

Trivet opened the folded note.

"'Deacon, come on fast and bring herd. Army is waiting. Con . . . con . . .'" Trivet shook his head. He pointed to the paper. "What's that word, boss?"

"Congratulations."

"'Congratulations on your . . . nup . . . nup . . .'"

"Nuptials."

"I got it, boss."

"Good. Now if you lose the note you'll remember it. Tell the deacon the army is here. Tell him Apaches are gathering in the hills and they're painted for war. Tell him I got women and whiskey waiting. Tell him anything you damn well please; just get him here with his herd."

Trivet looked doubtful, but he said, "I'll do my best, boss."

"Do better than your best. I need that beef."

After the puncher left, Harcourt poured himself a drink and lit a cigar. He wondered idly if the loco lawman was still alive after the beating he'd taken.

He doubted it. And if he was, well, it was only a minor inconvenience that Heap Leggett would clear up tomorrow.

He needed the timber from the town buildings to build his ranch house, where he'd install a permanent woman one day.

A crazy man was not going to stand in his way.

Chapter 6

This was the time, but not the place.

Sam Pace eased down the hammer of the Colt and laid the revolver on the desk in front of him.

He'd kill himself at the cemetery, near the spot where his wife and child were buried. Then all three of them could lie together for eternity.

They'd be a family again. Close.

Pace hurt all over and he was tired beyond measure. Blood crusted his scalp and face, and his body and legs were covered with purple and yellow bruises. A deep cut gashed down his thigh, angry and red.

The thought of the long walk to the cemetery unnerved him. He doubted he could make it that far in his present state. A little rest, then. To help his body heal. Tomorrow, at first light, he'd take the walk. His last.

He laid his head on his arms and closed his eyes. Within seconds he was asleep.

The candle on the desk guttered and shadows moved around the unconscious man. The wind sighed around the eaves of the office and rattled the wood shingles on the roof.

Over to the bank, a pair of hungry coyotes ate

their own kind, tearing flesh, crunching thin rib bones, their muzzles stained scarlet.

The ghost of Requiem, silver pale in the moonlight, haunted the darkness and spoke with a voice all its own . . . a whisper . . . a creak . . . a groan . . . a lament for the doomed and the damned.

The voices woke Sam Pace.

He sat up, his head on one side, listening intently into the night.

Was that what he'd heard? Was it really voices?

He rose from the desk and glided across the rough pine of the office floor, his bare feet making no sound.

Outside on the boardwalk, Pace heard a distant muttering . . . coming closer. The steady shuffle of feet on sand.

He smiled, raised his arms heavenward.

They were coming back! Dear God in heaven, the people had returned to Requiem!

Suddenly he was in the middle of the street. Waiting.

A cool wind sought the scrapes and cuts of his battered body, but he felt no chill, no pain, only a feeling of exaltation.

After three long years, the folks were coming back to their home.

Pace's eyes searched the darkness, and gradually they appeared, moving toward him like windblown leaves in the distance.

"Welcome!" he screamed, opening his arms. He wanted to hug each and every one of them. "Welcome home, folks!"

The people came closer, a grim, silent procession.

Pace backed away a step.

Where were the wagons, the mule teams, the children, and the outriders?

And where were the voices?

Pace felt a spike of fear. Something was wrong, something terrible.

These were not the people who had fled the town. *These were the dead returned from the grave.*

He took a step back, then another, his arms no longer welcoming, but crossed in a gesture of protection in front of his face.

Now, in slanted pillars of moonlight, he saw them.

Rotting flesh hung in tatters from their yellow skulls and their skeletal frames were covered in rags. Only the eyes were bright—glowing orbs of scarlet in bony sockets.

Women extended their arms to Pace, dressed in the gingham, flowered calico, and silk they wore when they died. But the worms had done their work. Gone were ripe lips, damp, ready for kissing. Breasts that in life had been pert and high, or had hung slack from childbearing, were gone and in their stead white ribs gleamed.

Pace screamed. Dear Christ, where was Jane?

The march of the dead did not falter, led by one he finally recognized, but only because the man held a tattered Bible to his chest. Around his bones the frock coat he'd been buried in flapped and his skull grinned, his eyes still afire with the light.

Pace shrieked. "Reverend Brown, send them back!"

His tongue long lost to worms, the preacher made no answer, though; like the rest of the unholy dead, he made an eerie moaning sound, keening like a winter wind.

Skeletal hands reached out for Pace and he smelled the close breath of rotting flesh and the moldering earth of the graveyard.

Burning eyes surrounded him, like monstrous fireflies in the darkness, and Pace tried to turn and run away, but he stumbled and stretched his length on the ground.

Suddenly he knew why they wanted him. It was not to drag him to the grave. It was not to beseech his help, or seek his counsel.

It was for a very different reason.

They were hungry!

Pace buried his face in the sand, moaning, as fingernails, taloned from long years in the earth, tore at the flesh of his back.

He screamed and screamed again.

Sam Pace woke with a start, reaching for his Colt even as he jolted upright in his chair.

His heart hammered in his chest and his eyes were wide with fear.

Gradually, breathing hard, he managed to calm himself.

It had all been a dream. Just a bad dream. The restless dead had not come for him.

Then he heard the scream.

A woman's scream.

A spiking cry of mortal terror.

Chapter 7

Jess Leslie was sure Sally had drowned in the swamp.

After they'd fled the deacon, Jess had stopped to rest in an ancient buffalo wallow, its sandy bottom well covered by brush and tall bunch grass. But Sally, terrified of the man, had kept on going. After a while, Jess heard men yelling, probably the deacon's sons, and then the shouts had faded.

At first she'd thought Sally had been caught. Only later, when she'd stumbled into the swamp, did she suspect that her friend had probably been sucked under.

Only Jess's discovery of a game trail through the marshland had saved her life, and now she stumbled into the darkness, gasping from effort and from sheer terror.

If she fell back into the hands of the deacon, he would kill her. He'd told her as much, claiming that he had once gouged a woman's eyes out after she'd cheated on him with another man, and only then did he put a bullet into her.

As the girl staggered onward, her way dimly lit by a wayward moon that cast more shadow than light, she heard coyotes yipping close by.

Too close.

Had she escaped the deacon only to be ripped apart by wild animals?

Ahead of her a narrow arroyo, stunted pines growing on its slopes, promised a road to . . . somewhere. If it wasn't a box canyon.

The moon's thin light offered little help and Jess plunged ahead, cactus and underbrush tearing at her dress.

The arroyo narrowed, then angled upward, and the girl was forced to all fours as she scrambled up the slope. Loose shingle rattled from under her feet, and brush ripped at her face. Her breath tore at her lungs as the going became steeper.

Jess felt herself grow weaker and she was afraid of blacking out and tumbling back down the rise.

Then a flitting shadow on top of the arroyo wall froze her in place.

There! She saw another, moving through the darkness like a wraith.

She recognized them for what they were—a pair of hunting coyotes.

And she was the prey.

Frantic now, the girl redoubled her efforts, clawing her way toward the top of the ridge.

Suddenly it was close to her. She saw a jumble of bare rocks, a few wind-blasted cedars and above those a scattering of stars. At last, she reached the top and crawled onto the flat, a stretch of grass studded with pines.

Jess straightened and plunged ahead, her scared eyes searching the gloom. She saw no sign of the coyotes.

The wolf always looks bigger in the darkness, and she told herself that her eyes had deceived her. Perhaps all she saw were a pair of frightened jackrabbits. Or it was a trick of the moonlight, casting shadows just to scare folks.

But she walked on quickly, glancing behind her often. She was only fooling herself. It had not been rabbits or moonlight back there at the arroyo.

An instinct, as old as humanity itself, warned her that she was being stalked.

After ten minutes of flight through the pines, Jess Leslie came upon a fast-flowing creek. She hiked up her dress and plunged into the cold water. She stopped once in the middle of the stream to splash water on her face and the back of her neck, and then waded to the other bank.

Now the ground gradually sloped away from her

and the pines gave way to wild oak and some scattered piñon and juniper.

Here the moonlight seemed brighter, though the land in front of her lay angled in deep shadow.

Then she saw it—a single pinpoint of light in the distance. A campfire maybe.

But how distant? It could have been one mile or ten. She had no way of knowing.

Jess heard a stealthy rustle in the grass behind her, and fear gave wings to her feet. She hiked up her skirts again and ran down the rise, heedless of the tree branches that slapped and swatted at her.

Then she was on flat grassland and right ahead of her was a town.

Sobbing her relief, Jess ran. She passed a darkened church and went on into the middle of the street.

She stopped in a patch of shadow cast by one of the false-fronted buildings, looking around her. The light she'd seen from the rise was straight ahead of her, throwing a pale yellow rectangle onto the street.

She prepared to run again, but the coyotes, heads down, growling, had cut her off and were now standing directly in her path.

Jess backed away, out of the shadow and into the moonlight.

The coyotes stalked closer, readying their attack.

She screamed for help—then she screamed again.

Her shrieks echoed through the silent town and came back at her. Mocking her.

Chapter 8

Gun in hand, Sam Pace staggered to the door and stepped outside.

Had he really heard a scream or had he dreamed it? The street was empty, but the scent of decay lingered. It was not the stench of the rotting dead. Surely it was the smell of the decaying coyote he'd killed the night before.

Pace, clutching on to the last shreds of sanity left to him, would not allow himself to think otherwise. He heard the scream again, a sharp, shattering shriek of fear. Hurt and stiff though he was, Pace ran in the direction of the sound.

Moon shadows slanted across the street, a series of light and dark rectangles, one after the other, cast by the false-fronted buildings. The wind rushed past his ears, urging him onward.

Faster. Faster. Faster.

Another scream, followed by a series of hysterical cries for help.

Then he saw them.

A pair of hunting coyotes stepped from shadow into moonlight like gray ghosts. They held their heads low, weight well forward, shoulders hunched, moving slowly, intent on the kill.

Pace saw a woman back out of a black rectangle into a patch of mother-of-pearl light, her gaze fixed on the predators, her face a blur of frightened white in the gloom.

He yelled and fired twice into the air. The coyotes spun on him, then stood for a moment, assessing the odds. Not liking the gunshots and the man running toward them, they scampered into the darkness, trailing alarmed yips behind them.

Pace sprinted toward the woman.

She saw him coming and screamed.

A naked man, more animal than human, charged at her through the malignant night.

The woman turned and ran. But she traveled only a few steps before falling flat on her face. She tried to rise, groaned once, and lay still.

"You fainted," Pace said, "and I carried you here. You're in my office."

He was no longer naked but had thrown on his tattered rags that Beau Harcourt's men had left lying in the street.

His marshal's star gleamed on his shirtfront.

The woman looked at him with wide, frightened eyes and fainted again.

• • •

Carefully, trying not to irritate the cuts and scratches on his scalp, Pace shaved away his long scalp locks of hair and watched them fall around his feet like black snakes.

He did the same with his beard, shaving close, but he spared his great dragoon mustache, once his only vanity, a Texas Ranger badge of honor that had taken him years to cultivate. This he trimmed and combed into a semblance of its old self.

The result he saw in the mirror did not please him.

His shaved head made him look older than his thirty years, and his blue eyes were glazed, distant, staring back at him like a rabbit hypnotized by a rattlesnake. He was painfully thin, his face tanned to a mahogany color by sun and wind, and he noticed wrinkles where none had existed before.

At least he wouldn't make the woman faint again.

Or so he hoped.

Pace stepped into the cell where the woman lay on his bed, an iron cot with a straw mattress. Both cot and mattress had seen better days.

She wore a pink gingham dress, stained and torn, and her scuffed shoes showed the wear and tear of hard travel.

Whoever she was, she was pretty, her eyelashes fanning over high cheekbones, a tendril of yellow hair falling across her forehead.

Her body was slim and shapely and she looked to be about seventeen, maybe younger, more girl than woman.

And she had a story to tell—if he could keep her conscious long enough to tell it.

Not by inclination a drinking man, Pace remembered that there was a bottle of Old Crow in his desk drawer that he'd kept for special occasions.

He smiled, revealing teeth that, despite everything, were remarkably clean and white.

If this wasn't a special occasion, then what was?

He poured a shot of the whiskey into a glass, returned to the cell, and shook the girl awake.

She opened her eyes and Pace said quickly, "For God's sake, don't faint."

To his relief, this time the girl looked at him without too much fear.

"Where am I?" she asked.

"In the marshal's office." Pace smiled. "I'm the marshal of the town of Requiem in the Little Colorado River Basin country. But, just so you know and so it won't come to you as a surprise, like, I'm tetched in the head."

To Pace's surprise, the girl rolled up her eyes and fainted again.

Chapter 9

Deacon Santee had chosen a pretty, peaceful place to make his camp.

His three wagons were drawn up next to a grove of wild oaks, and a treelined creek ran close by. Tall mountains, their slopes covered in pine, provided a dramatic backdrop and summer wildflowers grew in great profusion everywhere.

The deacon's cattle grazed on the other side of the creek, spread out over a square mile of grass, tended by the half-dozen vaqueros he'd hired along the Texas border.

"Well, Pa," Jeptha Santee said. "Have you reached a verdict?"

The deacon sat with his back against a tree, his Bible clutched in his hands. "I have," he said, "and it is a just one. The harlot will be chastised by the whip."

Jeptha grinned. "You want us to fetch her, Pa?"

"Yes, you found her in the swamp, so the privilege should be yours. Light the lamps, then bring forth Sally Anderson to meet her deserved fate."

Jeptha and his older brother, Enoch, sprinted to one of the wagons, disappeared under the canvas top, and emerged dragging a struggling, screaming woman between them.

"Let all here present witness her shame," the deacon said.

The girl turned her head to the deacon. "No! Please don't whip me!"

"You should have thought of that before you helped Jessamine Leslie run from the marital bed."

"Deacon, I'm sorry," Sally shrieked. "I'll do anything you want, but please don't hurt me."

As his grinning sons pulled the woman toward a tall cottonwood tree, the deacon said, "It's too late for sorrow. Now there is only my just vengeance."

Jeptha and Enoch, joined by their brothers Gideon and Zedock, laughed cruelly. Sally Anderson screamed for a while, then fell silent.

"She's dead, Pa. Ain't no use in whupping her no more."

Deacon Santee pointed his coiled bullwhip at the woman tied by her wrists to a cottonwood branch.

"See if she is faking it," he said.

"I don't need to, Pa," Jeptha said. "She's deader'n shit."

The butt of the deacon's bullwhip thudded against his son's cheek, leaving an angry red welt.

"You do as I say, Jeptha, and don't ever use that vile word in my presence again."

Jeptha, tall, rangy, dressed like his father in a broadcloth tailcoat and battered black hat, stepped sullenly to the tree, a hand to his cheek.

He grabbed the woman by the hair and wrenched back her head. He stared into her face for a few moments, then said, "She's gone, Pa."

"Gone much too soon," the deacon said. "She didn't suffer near enough."

Nine people had stood in lamplight and watched Santee flay the skin off the woman's slender back until the blood flowed.

Five were his wives; four his sons.

The deacon stepped in front of the women, who shrank against the sides of their wagons. He pointed with his whip.

"What do you see over there?" he said.

None of the women answered, fear stiffening their tongues.

Santee jammed the coiled whip under the chin of his youngest wife and lifted her pale face to his.

"Nancy, what do you see?" he said. He pointed with his whip. "Hanging from yonder tree, what do you see?"

The girl, sixteen years old and the deacon's fifth bride, was terrified. She said something in a whisper that no one could hear.

"Speak up," he said. "What do you see?"

Louder this time, the girl said, "Sally. I see Sally."

"And why is she hanging there?"

"I . . . I don't know," Nancy whispered.

The deacon threw up his arms, tilted his head back, and roared at the night sky. "She doesn't know!"

His prominent blue eyes popping out of his head, he ran down the line of women, stopping briefly in front of each one.

"Claire, do you know?"

"Leah, do you know?"

"Sarah, do you know?"

He halted when he reached the oldest woman in the group, a worn redhead with dead eyes.

"Maxine, tell me."

"Because she helped the Leslie girl escape your clutches, Deke."

"No!"

Santee shifted the whip to his left hand and backhanded Maxine across the face with his right. The woman fell, and he stood over her.

"Because she betrayed me!" he screamed down at her. "You hear that? She betrayed me."

The deacon stepped back and took a Bible from the pocket of his frock coat. He held the book against his chest and bowed his head.

He remained in that posture for ten minutes, and those around him stayed right where they stood, scarcely daring to breathe.

Deacon Santee cut an incongruous figure. He was dressed like a man of the cloth, a battered top hat on his head, yet under his coat two heavy Smith & Wesson revolvers hung from his hips in crossed gun belts.

He was small, skinny, pale, round-shouldered, thin-lipped, bald—and as fast and deadly with the iron as a rattlesnake.

Far off, among the wild oaks, an owl glided silently through the branches like a phantom and small things saw its fleeting shadow and squeaked and gibbered in the underbrush.

The lamps set around the cottonwood guttered in a breeze that pushed the dead woman's body back and forth and made the tree limb creak.

Finally, like a man waking from sleep, the deacon stirred.

He blinked, looked at the men and women around him, and said, "God has spoken to me. He said the woman betrayed my trust and my punishment was just. He said woe betide any other who is so inclined, for she will surely perish as did Sally, the whore of Babylon."

The deacon glared at his wives. "So saith the Lord. So saith me."

"Amen," Maxine said.

Santee stared hard at the woman for a full minute, but Maxine's face was empty of all but innocence and he let it go.

"You women get back into the wagons," he

51

said. "There will be no wedding feast this night."

The deacon watched his wives climb into the wagons, then said, "You, Gideon and Zedock, get back out there with the herd. Enoch, Jeptha, come here."

Jeptha, the deacon's youngest son, was a slack-mouthed youth of limited intelligence and filthy habits. Enoch, the oldest, was smarter and addicted to the historical novels of Sir Walter Scott and the works of Dickens. He also kept both volumes of Alexis de Tocqueville's *Democracy in America* in his saddlebags. He'd actually read the tomes several times.

Both he and Jeptha were vicious killers, and eager.

The deacon said, "I want you boys to find Jessamine. Bring her here so that she may feel the lash for her iniquity."

He stepped closer to his sons, his eyes blazing with the righteous fire of a witch-hunter. "This time I'll make sure she lasts longer than the whore hanging from yonder tree."

He pointed to the horse line. "Now mount up and go. If ye don't bring Jessamine Leslie back to me alive, it would be better for you two that you'd never been spawned."

Chapter 10

The rising sun slanted through the small cell window, throwing the shadow of its four iron bars on the floor.

"Ma'am," Pace said, "it's sunup. Maybe time you were awake."

The girl's eye fluttered, then opened, and this time Sam Pace kept his distance, standing with his back against the far wall.

"I'm the marshal," he said quickly, before she fainted again.

The girl sat up in the cot and touched fingers to her forehead.

"I feel so dizzy," she said. "Where am I? What town is this?"

"Requiem," Pace said. He stayed right where he was, afraid to move.

"The coyotes . . . ," the girl said.

"Yeah. I scared them away." He took a step closer to the cot. "Sometimes they'll do that if they're really hungry, attack a person."

The girl looked at him from head to toe, and her eyes widened, then brightened with alarm.

"*Uh-huh*. I look a sight, don't I?" Pace said, trying to throw a loop on her fear. "I had a run-in with some cowboys."

"You're the marshal?" the girl said, a gasp of disbelief.

Pace smiled. "What's left of him."

"What did you call this town?"

"Requiem."

"Strange name for a town."

"Well, it's a strange town."

"My name is Jessamine. Jessamine Leslie."

"Sam Pace. Right pleased to make your acquaintance, ma'am."

"And yours, too, I'm sure."

The girl rose and her skirts rustled as she stepped from the cell into the office.

Pace followed, carrying the glass of whiskey he'd poured earlier.

Jessamine stood at the window and looked out.

After a long while she said, "The town is empty."

"Should be," Pace said. "Requiem is a ghost town."

"Oh my God," Jessamine said. "It seems like I ran away from one hell and landed in another."

"It's just a town," Pace said.

He extended the glass. "Drink this. It'll make you feel better."

Jessamine took the glass in an unsteady hand, drained the whiskey in a gulp. She passed the glass back to Pace. "What happened here?"

"Cholera," Pace said. "Three years ago. It

took my wife and child and half the town."

"How did it happen?"

"The well water was poisoned."

"The well I saw last night? In the middle of the street?"

"Yes. I think it's still poisoned. I draw my water from the creek."

"I was going to drink from it," Jess said.

"I'm glad you didn't."

"Hell, so am I." The girl looked puzzled. "Why are you still here?"

"The people who didn't die up and left. But they'll be back, and I'll be here to greet them."

"When are they coming back?"

"I don't know. Sometime."

Jess's gaze searched Pace's face. "I don't know you from Adam, mister, and the whiskey has loosened my tongue, but I want to tell you something."

"Tell away. Call me Sam."

"I'll call you Sammy. I've always been partial to that name."

Jess moved from the window to the desk where Pace was sitting.

"It seems to me that you've stayed put right here for three years, but you've been running all that time," she said.

"From what?"

"Your memories. But you hope one day to recapture them and see things go back to what

55

they were. That's why you think the townspeople will return."

Pace sat at his desk, suddenly irritated. "That's not the way of it at all."

"The people might come back, but your wife and child won't."

"Don't you think I already know that?" Pace said. "I'm not that crazy."

"I think you are," the woman said.

"And you, Miss Leslie, what are you running from?" Pace said, anger touching his eyes.

"You can call me Jess. It isn't like we're kin, but 'Miss Leslie' doesn't sit real well with me."

"What are you running from, Jess? Your ma and pa?"

The woman smiled and shook her head. "What do you think I am?"

"A frightened, innocent young lady running from something . . . or somebody."

Jess laughed, a humorless yelp. "Innocent. Lady. Those are two for the book."

She perched on the corner of the desk and looked down at Pace.

Pace prompted the girl. "You got a story to tell, Jess."

"Are you asking me that as a lawman?"

"No, as an interested party. Well, maybe a little of both."

The woman brushed the stray tendril of hair from her forehead. "I never knew my pa, and my ma ran off with a traveling man. I've been selling it since I was fourteen; started off down Tucson way."

"I didn't know," Pace said, aware of how lame that sounded.

"How could you know, since I hadn't told you?"

Pace said, "Yeah, I couldn't know . . . about . . . that." He tried to smile. "By the way you look and such."

Jess gave him a long look, then said, "I ended up in a hog ranch in the Jacques Mountain country. Then the Apaches came and ran off all our livestock and burned the barn and smokehouse."

"And you fled?" Pace said.

"Don't ride ahead of me, Sammy."

"Sorry."

"The day after the attack a preaching man with loco eyes came in with three wagons. He spoke to Eli Shafer, the owner of the ranch—"

"Pimp, you mean," Pace said.

"Yeah, you could call him that. Anyhow, the preacher spoke to Eli and Eli spoke to me. 'Jess,' he said, 'I lost my stock, my barn, and my smokehouse an' money's tight, so you see how it is with me.' "

The girl uncorked the bottle and poured whiskey into the glass.

"Can't drink the water around here," she said.

She drank, then said, "I told Eli to say it plain and he did. He said, 'Jess, I done sold you to the

57

preaching man fer forty dollars and a side of hickory-smoked bacon.' "

Pace rose and walked to the window, a tall man, too thin, his slumped shoulders sagging under the weight of three years of deprivation and mad-ness.

The morning sun had washed away most of the night shadows, but the alleys remained rectangles of darkness and the aborning light added no luster to the store windows that stared back at Pace with blank eyes.

"What did the preacher man want with you?" he said.

That was a bad mistake.

Chapter 11

A man treads on dangerous ground when he casts even a hint of doubt on a woman's charms, and Jess Leslie was no exception to that rule.

"What the hell do you think he wanted me for, Sammy?" she said.

Pace recognized his mistake and tried desperately to undo the damage.

"I . . . yes . . . I understand. I mean . . . you being such a pretty woman an' all. Any man would . . . I mean . . ."

Her point made, Jess let him off the hook.

"The preacher's name was Deacon Santee and he wanted to make me his seventh wife."

Suddenly Pace was interested. "Would that be Deacon Santee from down El Paso way? Rides with four tetched sons just as ornery as he is?"

"You called that right, and when he's in the mood he lets them share his women. I learned that much the hard way."

"I thought Deacon Santee had been hung by the Rangers a while back."

"You thought wrong, Sammy."

"And you managed to escape from him? That couldn't have been easy."

"Well, I did, me and another of his wives. But in the dark we stumbled into swamp country and she either drowned or got caught, but I got lucky and made it to here. Then the coyotes came at me and the rest you know."

Jess stepped to the window beside Pace. "What do you see out there that's so damned interesting?"

"Just Requiem, and the morning light. It lies easy on the town, kinda like a blessing, but later, when the sun is full up, everything changes."

"Changes how, Sammy?"

Pace's smile was almost shy. "She shows all her scars and warps and wrinkles and it makes her look old and neglected and . . . sad."

"You're a strange one, Sammy," Jess said. "I don't think you're as tetched as you say you are, but you're a strange one. No doubt about that."

Pace's eyes caught and held the woman's gaze. "You don't think I'm tetched in the head, like them Santee boys?"

"No. You're nothing like them."

Jess looked around the office. "You got anything to eat, Sammy?"

"Yeah, a lot of cans back there. Jed Heaver, feller who owned the general store, just up and left with his wife and kids after the cholera started killing folks. He rode out in the middle of the night and left everything behind."

"And you've been eating from cans ever since?"

"This three year."

"No wonder you're as skinny as a lizard-eating cat." The girl stepped away from the window. "Let's take a look."

"Maybe you should rest," Pace said. "I'll get you something."

"Somehow I don't think I'd want to eat what you gave me, Sammy."

A jumbled pile of canned food was stacked up in a corner to the right of the cell door.

Jess kneeled and picked up the cans one by one, studying the labels that were still intact.

"Armour beef and gravy," she said. "A puncher told me about that."

Pace nodded. "It's not half bad. A little tough sometimes."

"Tomatoes."

"Kinda mushy."

"Beans."

"I eat a lot of those."

"Peaches."

"I like peaches."

Jess looked up at him. "Where do you do your cooking, Sammy?"

Pace was puzzled. "Cooking? I don't cook. I just open the cans and eat." He took a folding knife from his pocket. "Here, let me show you."

"Later, Sammy," Jess said.

She gave Pace a long-suffering, female look, then said, "Get some wood for the stove in your office."

"Damn, it'll get hot in here."

"It's already hot in here. We'll only keep the fire lit long enough to heat the food and bile coffee." She frowned. "That's if Jed What's-his-name left coffee behind?"

"Yes, a few sacks. I don't drink much coffee."

Jess shook her head. "They don't come much stranger than you, Sammy." She rose to her feet. "We'll have breakfast, and then I'll be moving on."

"You're leaving?" Pace said.

"That comes as a surprise to you?"

"Yes—I mean, no. I just thought you'd rest up some."

"Maybe you planned on having your wicked way with me, Sammy?"

Pace was shocked. "No, no. I never even thought about such a thing."

"Hell, I must be losing my touch," Jess said. "I saw you look at my tits, you know."

"Well, I mean, you're a very pretty woman."

"If you don't study me too close, Sammy. Now get me some wood and bring a sack of coffee. It'll be stale, but any kind of coffee is better than no kind of coffee."

Pace stepped to the office door, stopped, and turned. "You can stay, if you want."

Jess smiled. "Thanks, Sammy. But Deacon Santee will come after me, him and his sons. I reckon you've got enough problems of your own without adding mine."

"I'm still the law here."

This time the woman smiled like a mother who'd just listened to a boasting child.

"Get the wood, Sammy," she said.

Chapter 12

Heap Leggett sat his horse on a rise above the gently shelving valley that had once helped nurture the town of Requiem.

He kept to the cover of a stand of wild oak as he watched Sam Pace pick up pieces of wood from the street and boardwalk, shed skin from the decaying stores and saloons.

Leggett felt a vague pang of disappointment. As a matter of professional courtesy, he'd hoped he wouldn't have to draw down on the man.

Not too many years before, Pace had been something, his name mentioned whenever westerners gathered to talk of guns and the men who lived by them.

More lawman than a member of the gunfighting fraternity's restless breed, he had never been numbered among the ranks of the elite. But, as a named man, Pace had had to contend with more than a few hard cases who had gone out of their way to step around him.

Now, well, he was just a dead man haunting a dead town.

Odd, that, since Pace was still alive and Leggett didn't really want to kill him. But business was business and as far as Leggett was concerned, whatever had made Pace the man he was had died years before.

Beau Harcourt planned to tear down Requiem and build his ranch house on the site, close to the running creek.

Now Sam Pace stood in the way of progress and, unfortunate as it was, he must be forced to step aside.

Leggett, in no hurry, hooked a leg over the saddle horn and built a cigarette. He lit his smoke and watched Pace disappear into a shadowed alley.

The man appeared a few moments later, carrying a bundle of firewood as he walked toward the marshal's office.

Cooking something, Leggett decided.

But what the hell did Pace find to eat in Requiem? Rats maybe. Plenty of those around. He was surprised; figured a wild man like Pace would eat them raw.

A man who carries a gun, even a professional, will now and again tap the handle with his fingertips, reassuring himself that his weapon is still where it should be.

Leggett did that now.

Was Sam Pace still fast on the draw-and-shoot? He doubted it.

The man looked half dead on his feet. A sick man doesn't skin a fast Colt and he can't take his hits.

Sweat trickled down Leggett's cheeks and neck. The morning had grown warmer and the sun was burning the blue from the sky.

He lifted his watch from his vest pocket, consulted the time, and snapped the case shut again.

He'd wait another thirty minutes.

The condemned man deserved to enjoy his last meal.

Chapter 13

Sam Pace sat back in his chair, sighed, and built a cigarette, using dry, three-year-old tobacco. "Good stew, Jess. That's the first hot meal I've et in years."

"If you can call meat from a rusty can with tomatoes and beans a stew," the woman said.

"It came close."

"You're easy to please, Sammy. You'll make some lucky woman a good husband one day." Jess flushed. "Sorry, I shouldn't have said that."

"It's all right. Three years heals a lot of hurt."

"Do you still think about her, your wife?"

Pace nodded. "All the time. But it's not an open wound any longer." He smiled. "Well, except when I go crazy."

"You go crazy because you've been here by yourself too long, Sammy. You have to move on, as I'm fixing to do right now."

"I sure wish you'd stay, Jess. It's been real nice to have a woman around."

Jess rose to her feet. "Sorry, Sammy. I got to be—"

"Pace! Sam'l Pace."

Pace jumped up from his desk. He grabbed his Colt and walked quickly to the window.

Outside, a man stood in the middle of the street beside his horse, the reins in his left hand. He wore a gun and a bemused smile.

"What do you want?"

"Name's Heap Leggett, and I'm calling you out, Sam."

Pace had heard the name before, and who hadn't? Leggett was reckoned to be one of the best, and there were those who said he could shade John Wesley, if the two of them ever got down to it.

"Ride out, Leggett," Pace said. "I got no quarrel with you."

Leggett grinned and shook his head. "It don't work that way, Sam. See, Mr. Harcourt told you to get out of this town, and . . . well, you're still here, old fellow."

"You go tell Mr. Harcourt to come throw me out his own self if'n he wants me gone."

"That don't cut it, Sam. He wants you dead."

"And you're the one who's gonna kill me?"

"That's how she shakes out, Sam. I'm real sorry."

Leggett slapped his horse away from him.

"Come on out, Sam, and take your medicine like a man. It's gettin' mighty hot out here in the street and I've got the breakfast hunger."

Pace stepped to the door. Behind him he heard Jess whisper: "No, Sammy."

He walked onto the boardwalk, his Colt hanging by his side.

Leggett stood tense, ready.

"The warning was posted loud and clear when you were notified, Sam," he said. "You chose to ignore it."

"I don't want to kill you," Pace said. "Not today."

Leggett smiled. "Sam, there ain't much chance of that. Today or any other day."

"Walk away from it, Leggett. For God's sake, just leave it alone."

"My talking is done, Sam."

Leggett drew.

And died.

Pace's Colt had not yet leveled when a .44-40 bullet crashed square into Leggett's forehead, just under the brim of his hat.

Even with his skull shattered and his brain destroyed, a man can trigger a shot or two before the final darkness takes him.

Leggett, game to his last heartbeat, was no exception.

He thumbed off two wild shots before he fell backward and crashed to the ground, dust drifting around his lifeless body.

For a moment Pace stood where he was, stunned.

Then he heard heels on the boardwalk behind him.

Jess held his Winchester in her hands, smoke trickling from the muzzle.

"You killed him," Pace said.

"Seems like."

"Why?"

"Hell, Sammy, to save your life. And I wanted his horse and guns."

Pace kneeled beside Leggett. The gunfighter was as dead as he was ever going to be, his eyes staring at the indifferent sky.

He felt the brush of Jess's skirt as she stood beside him.

"He would've killed you, Sammy."

"Maybe. Maybe not. He didn't get his chance to prove it."

"Well, that's good for you and too bad for him."

Pace rose to his feet.

"Leggett didn't die in a fair fight," he said.

"He wanted to kill you, Sammy. So who cares what kind of fight it was?"

"I do."

Pace wrenched his rifle from the woman's hands. "You murdered him, Jess. You murdered Heap Leggett for his horse and guns."

"You didn't stand a chance against him, Sammy. He was way faster than you."

"You told me you killed him for his horse and his rifle and revolver."

"Yes, I know I did, and that's true. But I was also trying to save your life."

"Jessamine Leslie, I'm arresting you for the willful murder of Heap Leggett."

The woman's face was shocked. "You have no authority to arrest me, Sammy."

"I'm the marshal of this town."

"You're the marshal of nothing."

"A judge will decide that."

"Where the hell are you going to find a judge?"

"He'll be here. When the people come back."

Jess stared into Pace's eyes, searching for madness.

She found it.

Chapter 14

Mash Lake came down from the Padres Mesa country ahead of the four Peacock brothers, more troubles weighing on him than a sixty-eight-year-old man had reason to expect.

Thinking back on it, Lake blamed Mrs. Peacock, whoever she was, for his present woes.

Not content like a normal woman to have her babies one at a time, she'd squeezed out five at a single go, all of them boys.

A week before, in an act of great misfortune, instantly regretted, Lake had gunned one of them boys. Now the rest were on his back trail carrying hatred and coiled hemp.

That the killing was justified—a deck of cards has only four aces—was neither here nor there.

The Peacocks lived by a harsh code born of a hard land.

One of them was dead by the hand of another, and that called for a reckoning.

Around Lake the country stretched still and silent, hill country forested with cedar and pine. Ahead of him rose the purple peaks of the White Mountains, and somewhere beyond their sentinel ramparts lay the Mogollon Rim.

Lake had seen his last town five days before, his last ranch three.

By his own count he was missing at least six meals, but he still needed to put a heap of git between himself and the Peacocks.

All four of them boys were gamblers, as their brother had been, and they were good hands with the Colt's revolver.

And there was no backup in them. They'd keep a-coming, like a pack of starving wolves.

It is a comfort to a man to have a companion in woe, but Lake had none such.

Apart from himself, the only other visible living creature in the vast land was his yellow mustang. But the little horse was not much of a talker and pretty much kept his own counsel.

Lake calculated—rightly, it must be said—that the mustang didn't give a shit about his woes anyhow.

The day began its slow shade into evening and Lake rode under a candy cane sky when he came upon the town of Requiem.

From a distance, it looked like any other town he'd known, a place where no one would be glad at his coming or sad at his leaving.

He sat the mustang, lit his pipe, and studied the burg.

The town's only street was empty of people. More importantly, there was no sign of the Peacock brothers or their big American stud horses.

Truth to tell, there were no horses at the hitch rails, and, as far as Lake could tell, the street was unmarked by the passage of rigs and wagons.

He puffed on his pipe, a careful man thinking things through.

It was almost suppertime, so that explained the empty street. People would be home, settin' around the table or singing around the piano or whatever civilized folks did of an evening.

Lake had no way of knowing. He'd spent little time under a roof and none within the sound of church bells.

In the past he'd been an army scout, stagecoach guard, tin-pan gold prospector, lumberjack, railroad-track layer, cow-town peace officer, and for three months, before he'd given it up as a dead-end career, train robber.

Nothing he'd ever done was easy and nothing had come to him easy either. Some folks get life handed to them on a plate, but the plate had always been washed clean before it ever came around to Mash Lake.

He'd never lived with a woman who might have tamed him and helped him settle down in one place. He'd shared a bed with whores, of course, but they weren't the marrying kind.

Now, about to enter the seventh decade of his existence, life and the living of it had whittled him down to skin, bone, and whipcord muscle. He was tough, enduring, with no softness in him.

And he was a hard man to kill.

If he'd been asked, Lake could name four men who'd tried.

There was Bill Foran, a wannabe bad man back in the Nations. Foran had drawn down on Lake and it was the last mistake he'd ever made.

He'd outdrawn and killed Cedar Creek Hamp Lawson up Tin Cup way in Colorado, and three years later the Texas gunman John T. Walters, who'd called him out on Christmas Eve in El Paso over a two-dollar gambling debt.

Earl Peacock was the most recent, and at thirty years old he should have been of an age enough to know better than to draw down on a mean, grumpy geezer with the whiskey on him.

Peacock had pulled his gun after Lake spotted his crooked deal at Chuck-A-Luck.

The gambler had cussed him for a doddering old fool who didn't know his ass from a gin whistle and ordered him to skin iron.

An instant later the young man learned the hard way that in a belly-to-belly gunfight, age doesn't matter a damn.

Only one lamp burned in the town, a firefly in the darkness, and Lake thought that mighty unusual, since the night was starting to crowd closer and the shadows were stretching long.

But he needed a meal and a place to sleep, and both beckoned to him.

"The hell with it," he said aloud, to no one but himself, as is the habit of men who ride lonely trails. "Let's see what's shakin' in this burg."

He kneed the mustang into motion and headed into Requiem.

Later he would curse himself for not riding on and taking his chances along the Rim country.

Chapter 15

Mash Lake drew rein at the marshal's office, where a lamp burned, its two front-facing windows rectangles of orange light.

Around him the town lay dark and dead and only the prowling wind took any interest in his being there, sniffing him all over before moving on.

A horned moon began its climb into the sky, and the buildings along the street took on a ghostly sheen, their false fronts looming over Lake as though they were going to reach down and grab him.

Somewhere a door banged on its hinges. A feral dog barked. Blown sand sifted against the mustang's legs. Lake's saddle creaked. He heard his own breathing in the quiet. The dog barked again.

And suddenly the marshal's office went dark.

Lake's hand rested on the ivory butt of the Remington holstered across his belly.

"What the hell do you want? State your business."

A man's voice from inside the cabin—rough, unfriendly, and demanding.

"Lookin' fer a square and a bed for the night," Lake said.

"I got faith in this here rifle gun," the man said. "She shoots right where I aim her."

Deciding that the circumstances demanded a fast burnish of his bona fides, Lake said, "It's only me, ol' Mash Lake as ever was. Friend to all, enemy to none."

The marshal, or whoever he was, had the good grace to put a grin in his voice.

"Real true blue, ain't you, fer a night rider?"

"Lost my way," Lake said. "Seen your light. Pegged this burg as a place where I could get a bit o' supper an' a bed. Seems like I pegged it wrong."

"That depends," the man inside said.

"On what?"

"On me," the man said.

The office door opened and Lake saw a tall, thin feller walk out, then immediately step into shadow.

"Light," the man said. "And keep your hands where I can see them."

A moment's pause, then, "Mister, right now I'm nervous and when I'm nervous I get scared and when I get scared bad things happen."

Lake stepped out of the saddle, his hands high.

"No reason to be sceered of ol' Mash Lake, as mild-mannered a cove as you'll find in a day's ride in any direction."

"Around here, that don't cover a lot of folks," Pace said. "Come on in slow and grinnin', like you was bringing a fruitcake to Grandma."

Lake left his horse at the hitch rail and followed Pace's motioning rifle into the office.

He saw Jess and swept off his hat. "Pleased to make your acquaintance, ma'am," he said. "You must be the marshal's lady wife."

"She's my prisoner," Pace said. "Now shuck your gun belt and lay it there on the desk."

Lake did as he was told.

"Why are you in Requiem?" Pace said.

"Strange name fer a town," Lake said. "Makes me think o' death and Judgment Day."

He read the irritation in Pace's face and said quickly: "I'm just passing through, Marshal, comin' from one nowhere, goin' to another nowhere."

Lake scratched a bearded cheek. "Well, that ain't the whole story. I also got a hanging posse on my back trail."

"Why for that?" Pace said.

"Killed me a crooked gambler."

"Hell, gunning a base dealer ain't breaking the law. Nobody's going to blame you for that."

"Ah, well, his four brothers don't think that way. Narrow-minded gents, an' no mistake."

Lake's eyes strayed to the window. "They'll come for me, if'n they ain't here already."

Chapter 16

Beau Harcourt was worried. It was now full dark and Heap Leggett should've gotten back hours ago.

Hell, did the crazy man bushwhack him?

"Did the crazy man bushwhack him, boss?" Ben Trivet echoed Leggett's thought.

"Ain't likely," Harcourt said. "Heap is no pilgrim. He can take care of himself."

Trivet smiled. "Maybe he found himself a willin' woman."

"In a ghost town?"

His slow brain turning, Trivet said, "Maybe a ghost woman."

"Trivet," Harcourt said, "you're an idiot."

If the puncher was offended, he didn't let it show.

"You sure the deacon said he'd have his herd here tomorrow?" Harcourt said.

"Them's his exact words, boss."

"How does his herd look?"

"A bit winter-worn, but in fairly good shape. It's mostly young scrubs, maybe only a third of them beeves."

"The army will pay ten dollars a head, no matter what they are."

Trivet nodded. "The herd is good enough for Apache beef and most of them are strong enough to make the drive."

"When he gets here, you'll take all the hands and drive the deacon's herd to the Rio Puerco. You'll meet up with the army there."

"I take our thousand head along as well?"

"Of course. What do you think I'm gonna do? Leave them here?"

"I dunno, boss."

Harcourt sighed. "Get out of here, Ben. You're giving me a goddamned headache."

Heap Leggett preyed on Harcourt's mind.

Where the hell was the man?

There was nobody around faster than Heap, and sure as hell the crazy man couldn't shade him.

Or could he?

Finally, dark or no, he decided to go look for Leggett.

He saddled a good night horse, a slate-colored grulla, and told Trivet and the other riders that if he wasn't back by sunup to come looking for him.

The moon was full up, the sky ablaze with stars, when Harcourt took the trail to Requiem, coyotes yipping around him in the lilac and silver night.

He rode with his Winchester across the saddle horn, his searching eyes ranging far. Something about the moon-dappled darkness made him uneasy and the wind smelled like lead.

Was he going to find a dead man in a dead town?

Did Leggett discover, too late, that the crazy man was still good with the iron?

Harcourt spat away the bad taste in his mouth and the concern in his belly.

Ol' Heap had probably found whiskey in one of the saloons and gotten drunk.

Yeah, that was it.

He was drunk, damn him.

And loco Sam Pace was dead.

That was how it could only be. How it had to be.

Chapter 17

The slender sound of a flute spilled into the silence of Requiem, each note dropping like a silver coin into a crystal dish.

Inside the marshal's office, Mash Lake took the Apache courting flute from his lips and said to Jess, "Pretty, ain't it?"

The girl smiled and wiped a tear from her eyes with the back of her hand.

"It's beautiful," she said. "I'd fall for any Apache brave who played like that for me."

"A Mescalero courting flute's made from the bloom stalk of an agave," Lake said. "That's what gives it such a sweet sound."

"Play something else, Mash," Jess said.

"Well, on account of how you fed me and biled me up a gallon of coffee, I'll play something just fer you."

Lake brought the flute close to his lips. "This ain't Apache—it's Cheyenne—but it's another courtin' song an' right purty all the same."

"Mash, no more tonight," Pace said. "Miss Leslie is going to help me bury her hurting dead."

Lake's hands dropped and his shaggy eyebrows crawled up his forehead like gray caterpillars.

"Sam, now, you listen to me, boy," he said.

"Miz Jess here told me you was tetched in the head, and I didn't believe her. But when you talk about buryin' a dead man in the middle of the night, well, I got to believe your guitar ain't tuned right."

"I'm not going anywhere near that graveyard in the dark," Jess said. She shivered. "It's where the cholera dead are buried."

"I know," Pace said.

"People who die like that . . . walk."

"Sure do," Lake said. "Seen that my own self in El Paso town. Feller by the name of Husky Evans got hung for stage robbery. Day after they planted him, he walked right past the Butterfield office, still in his buryin' shroud. I seen him plain as I'm seeing you. His face was a kinda blue color and his head hung on one side on account of how his neck was broke. Thinking back, ol' Husky's ghost didn't look too good. Course, ol' Husky didn't look too good even afore he was a spook."

Lake laid a hand on Jess's shoulder. "Let the little lady stay here. I'll help you plant the dead man. Buryin' Heap Leggett is an honor anyhow. He was a fast man with the Colt's gun, the fastest west of the Mississippi. Everybody knew that."

Pace rose to his feet and shoved his revolver into his pants pocket.

"The little lady is my prisoner," he said. "Where I go, she goes."

Jess stood and put her fists on her hips. "Sammy, if you want me in the graveyard tonight, you'll have to drag me there."

"That can be arranged," Pace said.

"Why you in such an all-fired hurry to bury Heap anyhow?" Lake said. "You got a guilty conscience or something?"

"I didn't kill him," Pace said.

"I know. But he would've fer sure killed you, sonny. There wasn't a man alive was a match for Heap Leggett when he was on the prod. Jess saved your life and if you wasn't so tetched in the head you'd realize it."

Pace let that go and said, "The man needs a decent burying. But he's got friends and I don't want them to catch me in the cemetery come daylight."

"Then you and me will do it," Lake said. "Leave the girl out of it."

To Jess, Pace said, "You'll give me your word you won't try to escape?"

"Escape from what, Sammy? You? This ghost town?"

"I'll narrow it for you," Pace said. "Don't try to leave this office tonight."

"And if I do leave?"

"I'll hunt you down and bring you back."

Jess waited as a silence fell on the room. Then she said, "Hear that noise outside? It's coyotes, and I'm scared of them. I'll stay here."

81

Lake scratched his bearded cheek.

"Sounds like the dead calling to one another," he said. "Restless and sad, like."

Pace managed a smile. "Mash, don't scare Jess worse than she's already scared."

"Sure thing, Sam. I was just sayin', was all."

"Well, don't say it again. The night is always full of sounds."

He moved to the door. "Let's go. We have a burying to do."

Sam Pace and Lake dug the hole deep, then laid Heap Leggett to rest.

The two men stood beside the mounded earth, heads bowed, their pants flapping in a soughing wind as Pace said the words for the dead.

The moon drifted lower in the sky and gave center stage to the stars, and a thin light lay across the graveyard and silvered the canopies of the wild oaks.

After the wind tossed away Pace's final words like blown leaves, Lake looked at him and said, "Ain't much of a send-off to give a man."

"I got nothing better," Pace said. "I didn't know the feller."

"Then I'll try. I can always come up with something good to say about a dead man."

Lake dropped his arms in front of him, crossed his hands, then looked up at the night sky.

"Lord," he said, "please accept the soul of

Heap Leggett, the fastest man with a gun there ever was. Lord, you know he kilt Long Tom McCloud over to the Brazos River country, and Long Tom was a son of a bitch and reckoned to be the fastest gun west of the Mississippi until Heap came along and called him out. Give him credit for that, Lord, because Long Tom was a man who needed killin'."

Lake bowed his head and his voice rose.

"I recollect ol' Heap kilt Matt Agnew and John Judith and them two were polecats and would've been hung anyhow, so don't hold them killings agin him either. Same with that rancher feller Luke Battles, Lord. Remember him? He was what you might call a prayin' and psalm-singing man, so all Heap done was hasten him into a better world than this'n."

Lake shuffled his feet, like a man who knows he's overstayed his welcome.

"Well, I ain't got much left to say, Lord, 'cause I didn't know ol' Heap that well. But I'm sure he loved ladies and little children and the beasts of the field and said his prayers when he remembered."

Lake tossed a handful of dirt onto the grave. "He's all yours now, Lord, and if'n you ever have a range war with the Devil and need a fast gun, ol' Heap is your man. Amen."

Lake turned to Pace, his eyebrows lifting. "Well? Ain't you gonna say something?"

"About what?"

"Hell, how did I do?"

"I just wish his white-haired old mother could've heard that speech."

Lake's grin was lost in darkness.

"Damn right. Sam, I think you're a loco galoot, but you ain't as crazy as you make yourself out to be."

"But I am, Mash. Trust me, I am."

Lake put his flute to his mouth. "This is a lament for the dead called 'The Flowers of the Forest' and it's real purty. We'll see Heap off in style."

"Apache?"

"Nah. A Scottish feller waitin' to be hung teached it to me."

Lake played and the notes of the melody drifted in the wind . . . all the way to the listening ears of Beau Harcourt.

Chapter 18

Harcourt drew rein at the edge of town, and his eyes reached into the darkness. The street was deserted, the only light the rectangles of orange that were the marshal's office windows.

The notes of the flute fell around Harcourt like a ticking rain and brought him no joy and less comfort.

Pace wasn't a flute player, nor was Leggett. So who the hell was the musician? An element of the unknown had intruded on Harcourt's plan and he didn't like it one bit.

He shivered, but not from cold or fear. From something else. "Dread" was the word that described it, as though the black eyes of the night watched him, weighed him, and found him wanting.

The grulla pawed the ground, uneasy, impatient to be going. Harcourt quieted the horse and considered his next move.

The flute music came from the other end of the town, by the old graveyard. It would be dark there, way too dark for accurate shooting if it came to that.

Also, how many men were with Pace?

The answer dawned on him with terrible certainty.

The crazy man was burying Heap Leggett, and he'd at least one other with him, maybe more.

Despite the coolness of the night, Harcourt felt sweat bead on his forehead.

He couldn't chance a ride down there in darkness, into the guns of Pace and his cronies. It would be courting death.

Harcourt slid his rifle back into the leather and gave his situation some thought.

Finally he decided to go back to camp and

round up his men. Come dawn, they'd return shooting and end this thing once and for all.

But suddenly Harcourt saw something that brought a smile to his lips—a woman alone—and his course of action became crystal clear.

The door of the marshal's office opened and Jess Leslie stepped onto the boardwalk, the timbers creaking under her feet.

She stood for a couple of minutes, listening into the night, then turned and walked back inside.

A canny man lets his first impulse pass and acts on the second.

But Beau Harcourt was not a canny man.

He rode the grulla to the marshal's office, swung out of the saddle, and jumped onto the boardwalk. He kicked the door open and charged inside.

Jess made a dive for the Winchester in the gun rack.

Harcourt had a fleeting impression of the woman.

Young . . . thick yellow hair, huge eyes, a wide mouth, narrow waist . . .

He beat Jess to the rifle, grinned, then back-handed her hard across the face. The girl bounced away from him and crashed, unconscious, onto the floor.

Harcourt, a big man and strong, picked up Jess effortlessly, carried her outside, and threw her across his horse.

He stepped into the saddle and galloped out of Requiem.

As the grulla covered ground with its sure canter, the situation Harcourt had left behind amused him.

Obviously Pace was sleeping with the girl—and what man wouldn't?

Like a rat, the loon would wait until first light and then dart from his hole and come looking for her.

Out in the open he'd be easy to kill.

Chapter 19

"She skedaddled, Sam, just as you said." Mash Lake shook his gray head. "Little gal sure had me fooled."

"Seems like."

Pace glanced around the office; then his eyes caught and held on a patch of floor near the gun rack.

"Mash, come here, quick," he said. "Look at this."

Lake studied the warped timbers for a moment, then said, "It's blood. And there are other spots on the wall."

"Yeah. And I'm willing to bet that it's Jess's blood."

Lake's eyes wandered to the door. "What do you reckon happened?"

"Somebody came in here and took her, is what happened."

Pace rubbed a smear of dry blood between his fingers. "You ever hear of Deacon Santee?"

"Hell yeah. Everybody's heard of the deacon. I was told he got hung years ago down Texas way."

"He didn't. He's alive and well, sprightly and horny enough to take Jess as his seventh wife. But she ran away and when she stumbled on Requiem she warned me that Santee would come after her."

Lake whistled through his teeth. "The Deacon Santee I heard about, if it's the same one, ain't nobody to mess with, Sam. He's got a bunch of sons who are just as wild as he is and they're known for cuttin' up folks with bullwhips. The deacon his own self is pure pizen with a gun and he's as crazy as a loon."

The old man's eyes showed his concern. "Hell, Sam, he's even crazier than you, and that's sayin' something. Mind you, that only goes if this deacon is the original article."

"He's the original article all right. There's no doubt about that."

"What will he do to the girl?" Lake said.

"I think you know the answer to that, Mash."

Pace stepped to the window and leaned the top

of his shaved head against one of the cool glass panes.

"You know Jess is a whore?" he said without turning. "Been selling it since she was fourteen, she says."

Lake was old enough and experienced enough to take that in stride.

But he didn't answer, his face betraying nothing.

"I reckon there ain't a thing the deacon and his sons can do to Jess that men haven't done to her before," Pace said.

"Except kill her," Lake said.

"Right. Except kill her."

"What will we do, Sam?"

"Not we, Mash. There's only me on this one."

"What will we do, Sam?"

"She's my prisoner and I'm responsible for her. I'm going after her."

"And I'll ride with you," Lake said. "Whore or no, I like that little gal. She kinda grew on me, like."

"All right, if that's the way you want to play it."

"That's the way of it, Sam."

Pace crossed the room and opened a drawer in his desk. He took out a holster and cartridge belt.

"Leather is still supple," he said. "Even when I was at my craziest, I never forgot to oil them."

He filled the cartridge loops and shoved his Colt into the holster.

"We'll leave at first light," Pace said. He smiled.

"I'm not much of a hand at tracking folks in the dark. I don't see that good. You?"

"I've never done it, Sam. But we'll track better come morning."

Lake studied Pace from his scuffed, down-at-the-heels boots to the top of his bristled head.

"Know something, Sam? You'd look a sight saner if you ditched them rags you're wearing and got yourself some better-lookin' duds."

Pace glanced down at himself. "I guess that's what three years of living rough can do to a man. I look like a railroad bum, don't I?"

"You do an injustice to bums everywhere, Sam. You look way worse."

"Bring the lamp. There are a pile of men's duds in the general store, if they ain't been et by moths by now."

Chapter 20

Jeptha and Enoch Santee were camped north of Requiem in a stand of wild oak and pines tall enough to brush the stars.

The hunt for Jess had worn them out and they were dirty, tired, and mean enough to kill anybody or anything just for the hell of it.

"Damn it, Enoch, there it goes again," Jeptha said.

"I hear it."

"You reckon it's Apaches?"

"If they was close enough for us to hear their flute, they'd know we were here. And if they knowed we were here, we'd be dead."

"Then what is it?"

"I don't know."

"Ain't we gonna find out? Maybe the girl is with the flute player. Women cotton to . . . what do you call them?"

"Musicians."

"We got to find that damn . . . musician, Enoch. I'm pretty sure we'll find the girl with him."

"I'm studying on it."

Enoch, a huge, bearded man with matted hair hanging over the shoulders of his buckskin jacket, poured himself coffee, rolled a cigarette, then said, "This here's how I figure it—"

"Tell me, Enoch. If we don't find that uppity gal, Pa's gonna kill us."

"I'm about to tell you if you'll keep your big trap shut long enough."

"Sorry, Enoch."

The big man lit his cigarette with a brand from the fire, then said, "The way I figure it, that flute playing is coming from a cabin nearby. It could be a farmer and his old lady, and maybe the girl came on the place and she's still there."

"So we're gonna find out, huh?"

Enoch grinned, black teeth in a foul-smelling

mouth. "Sure we're gonna find out. I can smell women on the wind and I reckon we're gonna have us some fun before this night is out."

"What about their menfolk?"

"What about them?"

Jeptha thought about that, but couldn't find an answer that would not draw his brother's wrath.

In the end, Enoch answered the question for him. "We gun 'em, you idiot. Then we grab the women and do some humpin'."

"You got it all planned," Jeptha said, pleased.

"That's because I'm smarter than you and a sight more refined." Enoch rose to his feet. "Piss on the fire, then saddle up."

"Damn, it ain't a cabin; it's a town, Enoch," Jeptha said.

"I can see it's a damned town."

"But there's nobody to home."

"There's a light down there."

"If that's where the girl took shelter, we'll never be able to find her. We can't gun a whole goddamned town."

"Who says we can't? Kill a few people, and then tell the rest we'll kill a few more if'n they don't hand over . . . what's her damned name?"

"Jessamine, Pa calls her."

"Yeah, Jessamine."

"Do we wait for first light?" Jeptha said.

He was a youth with a slack mouth, a face

covered in yellow-tipped pimples, and the dull eyes of an ox.

"No, we won't wait. We'll ride down now and take a look-see. Catch them folks early when they're still half asleep and won't put up a fight."

"Enoch, can I do some of the killin'?" Jeptha said. "Seems like it's always you and Pa does the killin'."

Jeptha smiled. "Sure you can, boy. Do all the killing you want."

"A woman? I've never killed me a woman afore."

"Sure."

"I want a pretty one with bows in her hair, the kind that don't ever want to talk to me."

"Plenty of those around."

"Then maybe I'll make it two. I ain't never screwed a pair of gals with ribbons and gunned them when I got through."

Enoch kneed his horse into motion.

"There's a first time for everything, boy," he said. "Let's go."

Chapter 21

Sam Pace glanced at the star-scattered sky and wondered if the night would ever end. The thud of his boots sounded loud in the quiet and answering echoes bounced off the buildings he passed, adding thuds of their own.

The moon hung low in the sky and the surrounding mountains caught and held its gauzy light, drawing it over their firm peaks like a woman does her shift.

Pace was tired. His back ached and a headache threatened.

As though reading the younger man's mind, Lake said, "A while yet until sunup. Maybe we should grab your duds and then catch a few hours' sleep."

Pace smiled. "I guess a burying can tucker a man."

"Depends how deep the hole is," Lake said.

Like the rest of Requiem's survivors, the store owners had left in a hurry, leaving most of their stock behind.

Pace had no trouble outfitting himself with new underwear, socks, a pair of denim work pants, a blue shirt, and wide canvas suspenders.

The duds smelled of dust and age, but they fit pretty well.

He tried a new Stetson hat, but reckoned it would take years to break in and shape to his liking, and decided to stick with his old one.

As Lake predicted, Pace's appearance had improved greatly.

"Crackerjack." The old man beamed, looking him over from head to toe. "Boy, if'n I didn't know better, I'd swear you wasn't even tetched in the head."

• • •

Pace caught up Heap Leggett's stud near the livery stable and led it inside. He'd ride the horse come morning, but now he stripped off the saddle, pitched the big animal hay, then added a few oats he shook out from the bottom of a sack.

The theft of his Appaloosa rankled him, and its recovery would be part of the reckoning he'd exact on Beau Harcourt when the time came.

And the reckoning would come soon—right after he found Jess Leslie.

Pace stepped out of the livery and stopped.

Lake stood next to him and said, "Time for some shut-eye, Sam."

It was as though Pace hadn't heard him.

"Mash, you see anything strange about the graveyard?" he said.

"Not so I noticed. But hell, boy, it's a place for the dead, not the living, so it's gonna be strange."

"The ground was disturbed. In places it looked dug, or churned up from the bottom."

"I didn't see that."

"I had a dream," Pace said. "At least I think it was a dream."

"What did you dream about?"

"The folks who died of the cholera rose from their graves and walked in the street. I mean, right here, where we're at. And . . ."

A few moments passed; then Lake said, "And?"

Pace took a breath. "They were hungry, Mash.

As though being three years dead had given them an appetite."

"You mean they asked you fer food? Is that it?"

"No, but they were coming for me. To eat me. All them dead people."

Lake thought it through for a few moments, then said, "Sam, you ain't right in the head. A man who's tetched can have all kinds of bad dreams. Hell, even them who ain't crazy can have bad dreams."

The older man was silent for a while, then turned to look at Pace. He lifted the lantern he'd taken from the general store to see the younger man's face better.

"The wind lifts the sand and blows it around," Lake said. "That's what happened at the graveyard. Just the wind, boy. It was just the wind."

"But it seemed so real, that dream. Like they were right here, in the street, so close I could smell them."

"Well, a dream would seem real to a crazy man. It's the same kind of real that makes you think you're the marshal of a ghost town."

"I am the marshal. Nobody in Requiem ever said I wasn't."

"Sam," Lake said, "you just ain't right. And that's a pity because you're a real nice young feller when you ain't nuts."

"I didn't see them, the dead people?"

"No, you didn't, and that's the honest truth."

Lake put his hand on the younger man's shoulder, his voice taking on a sharp edge. "No more dreams about dead people, boy. Dreams take you nowhere, but a good kick in the ass will take you a long way. Understand?"

Pace smiled. "You mean if I dream about dead people again, you'll kick me up the ass?"

"Exactly. You've got the picture, Sam."

This time Pace laughed out loud, and it felt good. "Then I promise, Mash. No more bad dreams."

"Good, because at my age I don't think I can raise my boot high enough to kick a tall feller like you up the ass." He smiled. "At least, not as a regular thing."

Lake had night eyes and as they walked back to the marshal's office, he saw the two riders before Pace did.

And his old lawman's gut instinct warned him to treat them for what they were—trouble.

"Riders coming," he said. He stopped in his tracks and eased the Remington in its cross-draw holster.

"Trouble?" Pace said.

"That's what it shapes up to be, boy—trouble in pairs."

Unless a man is cavalry-trained to revolver-fight off the back of a horse, he'll always dismount to get his work in.

97

Enoch and Jeptha Santee were no exceptions.

The brothers stepped out of the leather, slapped their horses aside, and walked toward Pace and Lake.

They moved easily, with none of the horseman's stiff-kneed gait. Both men were smiling, self-assured, confident of their gun skills.

Pace took a single step away from Lake.

"On your left, Mash," he said.

He smiled. "Howdy, boys, looking for a place to rest up?" He waved a hand. "You got the whole town to choose from."

"Where the hell is everybody?" Enoch said. He noticed the star on Pace's shirt and added, "Lawman."

Lake answered for Pace.

"This here is a ghost town, boys. Nobody here but us two, poor old Mash Lake as ever was, and Marshal Sam Pace, who ain't right."

"Ain't right in the head, you mean?" Enoch said.

"Now, would he think he's the marshal of a ghost town if'n he wasn't tetched?"

"He do look tetched, with that shaved head an' all," Jeptha said. "Don't he, Enoch?"

"Shut your trap, Jeptha. I got business to attend to here."

"Here, hold up a minute," Lake said. "Enoch and Jeptha. I know them names. Ain't you young gentlemen good ol' Deacon Santee's sons?"

"What's it to you, old man?" Enoch said.

"Why, 'cause I'm a friend of yore daddy, fine, churchgoin' feller that he is. Surely you heard him talk about ol' Mash Lake and what a true-blue friend of his'n I am?"

"Pa ain't never mentioned you," Enoch said.

He looked on edge, hard in the mouth, his eyes lost in shadow.

"I'm looking for a girl," he said.

"None of them in this town," Pace said. "You want a woman, go someplace else where there are sich."

"I want one partic'lar woman, crazy man," Enoch said.

"Well, she ain't here," Pace said.

Pace knew he was being pushed and he didn't like it. A gunfighter's pride is a touchy thing. It's like a stick of dynamite. All it takes is a pushing man to light the fuse and it'll explode.

Enoch Santee was on the prod and he already had a match burning.

"Mister," Enoch said, "I say you're a damned liar."

"Here," Lake said, "that's a hard thing to say to a man."

"You shut up, you old coot," Enoch said. "I won't tell you a second time."

He turned his head slightly, his voice rising.

"Jeptha, search the place, starting with the marshal's office. The girl is here. I can smell her. These two idiots got her stashed somewhere."

"Stay out of my office, Jeptha," Pace said.

His voice held an edge sharp enough to shave with.

"An' if'n he don't?" Enoch said.

Pace would be pushed no further.

"If'n he don't, I'll kill him," he said.

Chapter 22

"Well," Mash Lake sighed, "I guess that just about tears it."

He was right.

"What will I do now, Enoch?" Jeptha said, hesitating with one boot on the boardwalk.

"You'll do as I say."

"Stay right where you're at, Jeptha," Pace said.

"Mister, I'm getting mighty tired o' you," Enoch said. "I'm ending this right now."

He went for his gun, a practiced, fast movement that blurred his right hand.

Pace was faster.

Enoch's gun was leveling when Pace's bullet hit him, high in the left shoulder.

Enoch absorbed the bullet shock, fired, missed, and took a step back, blood on his buckskins.

Beside him, Pace heard Lake shoot. He was vaguely aware that Jeptha had fallen to one knee, screaming, but was still trying to get his work in.

Enoch thumbed off a second round. But he'd been hit hard and was unsteady on his feet. His bullet plucked futilely at the left arm of Pace's shirt.

Pace steadied. Fired. Fired again. Two shots that sounded as one.

This time Enoch went down, sudden blood on his lips.

He sprawled on his back, chested a couple of great, heaving gasps, and lay still, all the life that was in him fled.

Mash Lake kneeled beside Jeptha, and Pace joined him.

The boy was dying, but he grabbed Lake by his shirtfront and whispered, "You got any pretty young gals with bows in their hair in this town?"

"A few," Lake said. "And they're real purty, an' all."

"I knowed they was here. I just knowed it."

"Did you want to meet a little purty gal?"

Jeptha nodded, smiling, his eyes fading. "Hell yeah. I wanted to fuck her, then blow her brains out fer bein' so damned uppity."

"Boy," Lake said, "you're a credit to the mama that bore you."

But Jeptha was already dead and didn't hear him.

Lake rose to his feet, his knees cracking. "Well, Sam, we know it wasn't the deacon took Jess.

These boys of his'n were on the scout for her."

"Seems like."

Lake gave Pace a speculative look. "You're good with the iron, Sam. As fast on the draw as any I've known."

"You throw some fast lead your own self, old man."

"I never throwed it at a feller more deserving than Jeptha. The boy was a sorry piece o' white trash."

"He was a mean one all right."

Lake stretched a crick out of his back. "Damn it, Sam, now there's more buryin' to be done."

"The hell there is. We'll throw a loop on their feet and drag them out of town. Them two Santee whelps don't deserve a proper buryin'."

"You're a hard, unforgiving man, Sam."

"I reckon. But only when I ain't crazy."

A thick mist arrived with the dawn, hugging the ground, and when Pace led the way out of town it looked as though he and Lake were riding through a gray sea.

"We ain't gonna find tracks in this fog," Lake said.

"It'll burn off when the sun comes up," Pace said.

Lake peered ahead of him, the mist curling around his horse. "So, where do we go in the meantime?"

"Pick a bearing, Mash. Any direction that takes us away from Requiem."

Lake, surprised, stared hard at Pace. "You ain't goin' sane on me, boy, are ye?"

"I don't know, old man. I could be. Maybe bein' crazy for three years is enough for any man."

"I don't know about that," Lake said.

"I don't know either," Pace said.

Chapter 23

One by one, Deacon Santee's straggling herd emerged from the mist. The slat-sided longhorns were flyblown, infested with the ticks that carried Texas fever, and barely able to stagger.

But the animals were still on their feet and to the army and the Indian agents, that was all that mattered.

Sure, the Apaches might mind such scrawny, diseased cows, but no one paid them heed anyhow.

Ben Trivet in tow, Beau Harcourt greeted Santee like a long-lost brother and immediately gave orders to start the combined drive to the Rio Puerco.

"I'm missing two top hands," Santee said, accepting a cup of coffee from the cook, "my sons Enoch and Jeptha."

"They ain't sick or shot or something?" Harcourt said.

"Nah, they're tracking a woman that ran from my camp on our wedding eve. My guess is they found her and are dallying with her someplace."

Harcourt, Trivet, and a couple of hands stared at Santee, Harcourt longest of all.

"I haven't seen her," he said finally, emphasizing each word, a warning to his men to keep their mouths shut about the woman in his tent.

Santee's skinny body shivered with a passion born of madness.

"If they haven't done so yet, my whelps will find her and return her to me," he said. "I'll cut the hide off the whore with a bullwhip and leave her corrupt flesh to be consumed by wild dogs."

Maybe Ben Trivet was just plain stupid, suicidal, or driven by a misplaced sense of male gallantry.

Whatever the reason, it was about to cost him his life.

"A Texas gentleman doesn't talk about a woman that way," Trivet said, his cheekbones red. "And I mean any woman, even a whore."

Harcourt spoke into the tense hush that followed, trying to head off trouble.

"Ben, you and the others get the herd moving," he said. "The army won't wait."

"Hold up, Ben," Deacon Santee said. His eyes glowed, like those of a cat stalking a mouse.

He took a step toward Trivet and brushed his frock coat away from his guns. He spoke to the puncher, his voice iced.

"You dare to show me such disrespect"—he waved a hand—"in front of my sons and my women? How dare you imply that I'm not a gentleman."

"Apologize to the deacon, Ben," Harcourt said. He looked at Santee. "He meant no disrespect." Then he attempted what he hoped was a disarming smile. "It's too early in the morning for a killing, Deacon."

Trivet felt the breeze cool on his face. He heard the babble of the creek as it bubbled over blue river stones, the rustle of jays quarreling in the wild oaks, and he saw the play of sunlight in the mist.

He was twenty-five that summer, healthy, strong, and he'd formed a vague plan to start his own ranch one day with a pretty wife at his side.

Right then he was scared and he didn't want to die.

It's good for a man to have pride, but now and again it will turn around and spit in his face.

As it did now.

Trivet, aware that other men watched, found himself backed into a corner. He knew he couldn't show fear or any hint of git, so he did all he could do—reach down into himself and find his cojones.

"I ain't apologizing, Deacon, for what I think," he said. "A man's got a right to his opinion."

Santee nodded, his pinched, malicious face grave. In a somber voice, as though giving a sermon from a pulpit in hell, he said, "Then the slanderer must die, for that is the law of God. Verily, he shall be destroyed for his iniquity and his bones scattered by wild beasts."

"No!" Harcourt yelled.

The fraction of a second it took Harcourt to utter that exclamation matched the speed of Santee's draw.

The deacon skinned both guns and the shots sounded as one.

Trivet's face went slack and there was a strange, luminous shock in his eyes. Hit twice in the chest, he fell on his knees, his gun coming up, and Santee, grinning, shot him again.

Trivet died in that position, on his knees, all ready to meet his God.

But the deacon would have none of that.

He lifted his boot, kicked Trivet in the chest, and sent his body jerking backward.

"Fair fight," Santee said. He was looking at Harcourt.

"Fair fight," Harcourt said, the words bunching in his throat.

But it had been cold-blooded murder and the rancher knew it.

Trivet was no gunfighter. He was a dead

106

man the moment he spoke up about the woman.

Still, the deacon could've let it go, laughed it off, and no harm done.

But he hadn't.

And Harcourt knew the reason: The man felt the need to prove how fast he was with the iron.

Damn it, why?

The answer to that question brought realization, and with it came a chill that iced Harcourt's belly.

He'd thought of the deacon as nothing more than a business associate, albeit a crooked one, but basically harmless.

Now all that had changed.

Santee had shown himself to be something else entirely, a man more ruthless, callous, and dangerous than Harcourt ever could have imagined.

He looked at the deacon reloading his guns, and a sense of foreboding filled him, like a man who hears the tolling of his own funeral bell.

Chapter 24

The herd was ready to move out, but the deacon took his sons Gideon and Zedock aside and led them close to his wagons.

"You know what to do," he said. "The Mexicans

I hired are all good with the iron and they'll back your play."

Santee bunched a fist into Gideon's shirt, pulling him close to his own scowling face.

"I want all the Harcourt hands dead, you understand? Shoot them. Then shoot them again. Let not one of them escape you."

"Is this afore or after we sell the herd?" Gideon asked.

He was small and thin like his father, and every bit as spiteful and mean. Even whores stayed clear of him after he marked a few, and dogs ran from him in the street.

"Damn it, where is Enoch when I need him?" the deacon said. "After, you idiot. After you get the money from the army quartermaster."

"We come back here, Pa?" Zedock said.

The deacon let out a slow hiss of exasperation.

How the hell had he sired idiots like these?

"I went over all that already. First you send a rider on a fast horse to tell me you made contact with the army. Then you head back here your own selves with the money." He laid on some sarcasm. "I'll be the only man standing, so even you two will be sure to recognize me."

"We'll do as you say, Pa," Zedock said. "You can count on us."

"Let's hope so," the deacon said. "If you foul this up, don't come back because I'll kill you on sight."

He lashed at the two young men with his riding crop.

"Why the hell are you standing there with your mouths hanging open? Mount up and git going. And make sure you keep the Mexicans in check. I'll deal with them later."

Santee watched the herd move out, the cattle drifting through a cloud of yellow dust.

He smiled, happy at the way things had worked out.

There were seven Harcourt riders and seven of his own—his two sons and five Mexicans fresh off the Texas border, where they'd played hob, robbing, raping, and killing.

Killing Trivet had evened the odds and he was confident Gideon and Zedock could do the rest.

He looked around the camp.

A couple of Harcourt's punchers were holding the remaining half of his herd in a box canyon three miles to the south. Only two of his men were in camp, the cook and an older hand who had pleaded sickness from an attack of piles.

When the time came he'd handle those two himself.

As for Beau Harcourt, he was sulking in his tent. The deacon smiled. Even the sight of somebody else's blood had been too much for him.

Now the man expected a share of the army

money and that made the deacon's smile stretch into a grin.

He'd pay Harcourt off all right. In lead.

Santee's wagons were parked under a stand of pine and wild oak and he watched his women walk back and forth, their hips swaying. He walked in the direction of the wagons.

But he stopped in his tracks when he saw the four riders coming in.

Damn it, even at a distance, they looked like specters of death on horseback.

Santee's hands dropped to his guns.

Chapter 25

Sam Pace and Lake rode northward, the broad land lying open before them. The mist had lifted and the ten-thousand-foot-high peaks of the White Mountains were now visible to the east, their pine-covered slopes motionless, drowsing in sunlight.

"See it, Sam?" Lake said, his sharp old eyes reaching out over the dry grassland.

"Yeah, I've been studying on it for quite a spell. It ain't smoke, is it?"

"Dust. Something mighty big kickin' it up."

"The deacon's herd?"

"Seems like. Two thousand head of cattle

make a heap o' dust in their passing."

Pace's mind was working. Had the deacon snuck into town and taken Jess? It hardly seemed likely, but it was possible.

Lake said aloud what Pace had been thinking.

"Maybe he's got Jess," he said. He amended that. "I mean, your prisoner."

"Well, she isn't my prisoner right at this moment," Pace said, irritated. "Now, is she?"

"Sorry, Sam," Lake said. He smiled. "I was only sayin'."

"Well, don't say it, Mash. It's starting to annoy the hell out of me."

"That's 'cause you're tetched, boy. Makes you fly off the handle real easy."

Pace let that go. Now was not the time to discuss his sanity or his lack thereof.

He drew rein and stared at the dust cloud.

"What the hell do we do now?" he said. "We can't go charging into a cattle herd that's kicking up dust, looking for a girl who might be there or might not."

"No, we can't, Sam. Anyway, if it is the deacon and we go anywhere near his woman, he'll shoot us off'n these horses quicker'n scat."

After bowing his head in thought for a few moments, Pace straightened and said, "Well, there's nothing that says we can't take a closer look."

"What fer a closer look?"

"Because I want Jess back, and right now I can't think of anything else to do. Can you?"

"Well, we could return to Requiem."

"For what?"

"To plan our strategy."

"Damn it, we don't have a strategy."

Lake didn't take time to think about it longer. "All right, then, let's take a closer look." He grinned. "Maybe we can cut your prisoner out of the herd without the deacon taking pots at us."

"Mash," Pace sighed, "there are times when you try a man's patience. You surely do.

"We won't waste time following the herd. We'll ride on ahead and see if we can figure where it's headed."

"Seems as good a plan as any," Lake said. He was silent for a moment, then said, "Here, Sam, you think the deacon might be throwing in with the Harcourt feller?"

"I've been studying on that and it seems likely."

"Run their herds together and start a ranch?"

"Maybe so."

"Strange, that."

"Why?"

"On account of how the deacon ain't a one fer sharing. That's if everything I've heard about him is true."

"I guess there's a first time for everything, Mash."

"Yeah, I suppose stranger things have happened.

Could be the deacon plans to go respectable, settle down as a rancher, like."

"You believe that?"

Lake smiled and shook his head. "Not a word of it."

Chapter 26

Pace and Lake bypassed the herd by riding well to the south. They kept to the timbered valley country where there was no chance of getting skylined on a bare ridge.

The day was hot, the sun well up in the sky, and there was no cloud. Even among the pines and wild oak, the heat pounded at the riders mercilessly, and their shirts were black with sweat.

Only the mountains looked cool, green and lilac in the distance.

Pace kept an eye on the dust cloud to the north.

The cattle seemed to be moving steadily, driven close and hard, but at noon the dust halted and Lake reckoned the herd had bunched up to drink the silty, riffled waters of Silver Creek.

Pace led the way east for three miles, then swung due north again. He and Lake were now well ahead of the deacon.

After another fifteen minutes, they rode through a stretch of brush country, then into pines that led all the way to the top of a rocky hogback.

Pace drew rein. He was hot and irritated, and there was enough scare in him to tighten his throat when he spoke.

"Hell, Mash," he said, "we're riding blind. We could be heading right into a bellyful of lead."

"Figured that my own self a while back," Lake said.

"But it don't scare you none?"

"Scares me plenty. Anything to do with Deacon Santee scares me plenty."

Pace studied the crest of the rise. If he and Lake dismounted and worked their way to the top, they could get the lay of the land and the likely destination of the herd.

He ran his plan past Lake and the oldster nodded. "Suits me. I got nothing else to do this morning."

Pace tied their horses in a small hollow surrounded by brush where they'd be out of sight. Then he and Lake began their climb.

The slope was a lot steeper than it looked from the flat and they had to climb part of the way on all fours, to the delight of the little claret cup cactus that hid in the grass and ripped mercilessly at their hands.

Lake vented his lungs a couple of times when spines stung him, until Pace hushed him into an irritable silence.

Their bellies hugging the ground, Pace and Lake looked down onto a wide bench that sloped upward a few feet from an S-shaped creek.

A sizeable herd grazed on both banks of the stream and along the edge of a pine and oak forest that bordered the bench to the west.

A second herd that looked to be about a thousand strong was bunched several hundred yards from the creek, the punchers keeping the cattle closed up tight.

But what drew Pace's attention was the tent pitched in one bend of the S. Nearby was a camp-fire and at a distance a couple of dozen glossy horses cropped grass.

"Jess could be in the tent," Lake said.

Pace nodded. "It's a possibility."

"How we gonna play it, Sam?"

"We wait and we watch and hope something breaks."

Lake turned on his right side, his eyes scanning the horizon.

"Dust cloud is close," he said.

"Yeah, this is where the deacon is headed, sure enough. You were right, Mash. He's throwing in with Harcourt and his bunch."

Mash gave a slow grin. "Something tells me it won't be a happy marriage."

From their perch above the bench, Pace and Lake saw the deacon's herd arrive. Later they watched the death of Ben Trivet and the departure of the combined herds and could make no sense of either.

Lake pegged Trivet's killer as Deacon Santee.

"Has to be him," he said. "Ain't nobody else hereabouts wears a frock coat, a stovepipe hat, and shucks a gun that fast."

Pace nodded. "He's fast all right, real slick on the draw-and-shoot."

"He ain't a man to mess with, Sam."

"I just came to that conclusion my own self," Pace said.

A few minutes before noon, appearing out of dust and a shimmering haze, rode four men in black, sitting tall on blood horses.

Lake watched the deacon walk toward them, then turned to Pace.

"The Peacock brothers," he said. "I left a broken trail behind me, but they tracked me down. Now they know fer sure that I'm somewhere in this neck of the woods."

"All right, so now we got another bridge to cross," Pace said.

"I got a bad feeling about . . . ," Lake began. His voice faltered to a halt.

"Don't say it, Mash," Pace said. "They're only men, like the rest of us, and I've seen their kind before. Ever catch sight of the Earp brothers? I reckon them and the Peacocks are cut from the same cloth."

Lake was no coward. He'd proved that often enough in the past. But suddenly he looked old and tired, a man who'd long before played out his string.

"Sam, you ever hear tell of the angel of death?" he said.

"I heard a tent preacher talk about that one time."

"Well, the angel just spoke to me."

A shiver ran down Pace's spine. "There ain't no angel of death, Mash. It's all in a man's mind."

As though he hadn't heard, the old man said, "I'm wrote down in the angel's book in letters of fire. That's what he tol' me, plain as day."

Pace looked at him. "Mash, get away from here. Ride south for the west Texas country where you have friends."

Lake smiled. "Too late for that, Sam. I'm like the ranny who jumped off the cliff. No matter how much he regretted it on the way down, he knew there was no goin' back."

Pace moved his gaze to the men talking with the deacon.

And it dawned on him with terrible certainty that he was looking at four ambassadors from hell.

Chapter 27

Beau Harcourt walked out of his tent, leaving a tied-up Jess Leslie behind, and was taken aback by his visitors.

Four men sat tall, gaunt horses that stood heads hanging, dusty, and trail-worn.

But it was their riders that drew and held his attention as something ancient and reptilian in his brain warned him of danger of a kind he'd never encountered before.

The four men looked alike, their narrow faces pale and sunken, as though they were being eaten by the same death cancer.

They affected the dress and manner of the frontier gambler, black frock coats and pants and boots of the same color. Despite the heat, they wore high celluloid collars and string ties. Their hats were low-crowned and flat-brimmed, gold bands adding the only color to their somber outfits.

Each man wore a blue cross-draw Colt and had a Winchester booted under his right knee.

Harcourt had been around gunfighters before, men like Heap Leggett who were among the best, but he'd never encountered four like these.

Something . . . strange emanated from the

men. It reached out to him with tentacles. Something more than danger; something more than menace; something akin to evil; something . . . demonic.

The day was bright, the sun hot, yet Harcourt felt darkness come down on him, as though he stood in the shadow of a gallows.

"These gentlemen are the Peacock brothers from up in the Padres Mesa country," Deacon Santee said. "I didn't get their given names."

"Because they don't matter," one of the riders said. His eyes were green, like the sea off a rocky coastline. "Tell your friend the urgent nature of our business."

"They're hunting a man, Beau," the deacon said. "Feller who goes by the name of Mash Lake. You seen or heard of him?"

Now Harcourt felt four pairs of green eyes on him and he didn't trust himself to talk.

He shook his head.

"Figured that," the deacon said. "Like I told you boys, there ain't many strangers come calling around these parts."

Then a strange thing happened that shook Harcourt and even made the deacon's eyes bug out of his head.

The brother who sat his horse at the left of the line moved his mouth as though he was forming words. But he didn't utter a sound.

One of the others spoke for him.

"If you boys are lying to us, it would be better for you if you'd never been born."

The Peacock who'd spoken aloud saw the stunned look in Harcourt's face and said, "My brother can't talk, so I do his speaking for him."

The deacon, maybe braver or more foolish than Harcourt, said, "Damn it all, how is that possible?"

"I know what he wants to say and when he wants to say it."

The dumb Peacock's mouth moved again.

"What's in the tent?" his brother said.

"Nothing!" Harcourt said.

Too quickly.

The Peacock brothers stared at him and Deacon Santee gave Harcourt a surprised look that quickly turned hard and measuring.

Harcourt tried to cover up his gaffe. "I've got private papers in there is all."

"We won't touch your private papers," said a brother who had been silent until then. "Only the man who calls himself Mash Lake is of interest to us."

He kneed his horse forward to the tent, leaned out of the saddle, opened the flap, and looked inside.

After a few moments he swung his horse around and said, "Lake isn't there."

Harcourt exhaled his relief. Tension drained out of his belly like a beer-drinking man taking a piss.

It seemed the Peacocks were intent on the man

called Lake. Nothing else, including the sight of a naked woman on a cot, mattered to them.

Emboldened now, Harcourt said, "There's a ghost town to the south of here. Seems a likely place for a man to hole up for a spell."

The brothers said nothing. They swung their horses, trotted away, and didn't look back.

After they'd gone, Harcourt felt the air thick and hard to breathe, as though the Peacocks had polluted it by their very presence.

Chapter 28

From his perch on the rise, Pace watched the Peacock brothers leave. Beside him Lake was unusually quiet, his breath coming in short, quick gasps.

Was the old man frightened?

That seemed unlikely. He'd stood his ground and got in his work during the fight with the Santee boys and there had been no backup in him.

He said the deacon scared him, but then the deacon scared everybody, Pace included.

It had been the sudden appearance of the Peacock brothers that had tipped the scales and weighed the old man down.

Pace searched his brain for something reassuring to say, found nothing, and settled for "That

Peacock you shot, did he look like them fellers down there?"

"Spittin' image," Lake said. "He had a skull for a face and green eyes that looked right through a man." He rubbed the back of his hand across his mouth. "The feller needed killin' all right, but why the hell did I have to be the one that done it?"

"Because you was there, Mash."

"Yeah, but I could've been someplace else, just as easy."

"Hell, he drawed down on you."

"Nah, he didn't. He had his hog leg in his hand and was shoving it into my face, like, cussin' me out fer being a loco old coot. Well, by and by I got tired o' hearin' that and I drawed and gunned him. Surprised the hell out of the Peacock feller. He figured I was scared shitless and he wasn't expectin' nothin'.'"

"Then his brothers came after you."

"Right. And the Peacock boys don't come at you one at a time. They hunt and kill in a pack, like wolves. Hell, I heard they even howl at the moon like wolves and eat their meat raw."

Pace's eyes were following Harcourt's movement as he and the deacon walked toward the wagons.

"A man hears a lot of things from other men," he said.

"Some of them even true," Lake said, without a hint of a smile.

●●●

A few minutes passed. Among the wild oaks the jays were too hot to quarrel, but crickets sawed love songs in the long grass and a rustling breeze added a descant.

There was a gray tinge to the sky that could signal a weather change, but the sun burned strong and there were no clouds.

After a silence, Pace said finally, "Jess ain't in the tent, so that means she ain't here. Unless she's in one of the deacon's wagons."

Down on the flat, Harcourt was talking to Santee and there was a woman with them—not Jess, but one of the deacon's wives.

Even at a distance, Pace thought Santee seemed tense. His body posture was stiff and his hand movements were quick and jerky.

Could it be that his killing of the Harcourt drover was troubling him?

Pace doubted it. If all the talk was true, the man had killed so often in the past, the death of a nameless, faceless cowboy would hardly disturb him.

Then it had to be the Peacock brothers. But why would the deacon care?

Lake gave Pace no more time to ponder the question.

"Lookee," he said. "The tent."

Pace moved his gaze to the tent. He noticed nothing out of the ordinary.

"What did you see?" he asked.

"Canvas moved. There's somebody in there."

"One of them Peacock boys looked and saw nothing."

"He didn't see what he wanted to see," Lake said. "A feller by the name of Mash Lake. The woman didn't interest him."

"Jess?"

"My bet."

A minute ticked by, and then Jess Leslie made her run.

The tent flap triangled open, and the woman stepped outside.

She glanced quickly at Harcourt and the deacon, then hitched up her skirts and bolted for the shelter of the trees.

"Hey! Stop!" Harcourt yelled.

He drew his gun and fired.

Pace saw an exclamation mark of dirt spurt near Jess's feet.

She kept on running. Still with a hundred yards of open, broken ground to cover.

"Well, shit!" Pace said. "Now the hog fat's in the fire."

He pulled his Colt and fired at Harcourt, scaring the man badly enough that he dived for the cover of a clump of brush. Beside him the deacon did the same.

Now Lake was shooting.

The range was too great for accurate revolver work, but he and Pace bought Jess precious time.

The woman was almost at the trees.

Pace thumbed off a couple of quick shots, then ducked as a bullet racketed through a low-hanging oak branch inches above his head.

Lake was firing steadily, not scoring hits, but keeping Harcourt's and the deacon's heads down when it mattered.

He turned to Pace, his face revealing concern. "Let's git the hell out of here, Sam. The shot that near took your head off was the deacon's. He's getting the range, damn him."

A quick glance told Pace that Jess had reached the trees. Needing no more urging from Lake, he bellied down the slope a couple of yards, then got to his feet and ran.

He and Lake reached the hollow where they'd left the horses, and mounted. They galloped away from the ridge and bullets followed them.

Pace turned and saw the deacon on the rise, two-handing his revolver at eye level. The man was screaming obscenities, dancing a mad little jig, but he made no hits, though a couple of his shots split the air close to Pace's head.

"Sam," Lake said when the danger had passed, "don't let's ever do that again."

"Suits me just fine," Pace said.

He thought about the deacon.

Even at long revolver range, he'd come mighty close. In a spitting-distance gunfight, he'd be deadly.

It was the kind of worry guaranteed to keep a man awake o' nights.

Chapter 29

Deacon Santee was in a killing rage.

Beau Harcourt had kidnapped his woman, he'd been shot at, and when he'd dived for cover he'd landed belly first in a steaming pile of cow shit.

Harcourt realized the danger he was in and desperately tried to rewrite the history of the last few minutes.

"Hell, Deacon," he said, "I was saving her for you."

"Humping her for me, you mean?"

Santee looked small and narrow and his eyes were ugly.

"I swear I didn't touch her," Harcourt said. "I was saving her for you, Deacon. I figured when we got paid for the herd, I'd loose her to you, as a celebration, like."

Santee's eyes glowed with blue fire, and Harcourt knew he was now walking the edge.

"I can't trust you anymore, Harcourt," the deacon said. "Verily the traitor shall perish in the flames and the demon ravens will peck out his lying eyes."

"I didn't taste her, I swear," Harcourt said. He bowed his head in mock humility. "All I did was try to please you, Deacon."

"Where are my sons?"

Santee's question took Harcourt by surprise.

"Why . . . why, they're with the herd."

"My other sons, Jeptha and Enoch. You had the woman here, so their search for her was in vain. My boys should be back by now. Where are they?"

Harcourt shook his head. "I don't know."

"Did you have them murdered to get to the woman?"

"No, Deacon. I found the woman in the ghost town."

"Did you kill my boys, Harcourt?"

"No, no. I swear on the Bible I didn't."

"I hope you're telling the truth. If my sons have been killed, better that their murderer had never been born. Better he tie a millstone around his neck and cast himself into the depths of the sea."

The oiled blue metal and yellowed ivory of the deacon's guns caught and held Harcourt's attention.

How fast was he? Hell, Harcourt had seen his draw.

He was faster than anyone could imagine.

He'd answered his own question.

But he consoled himself with one thought: A

bullet in the back was the ultimate equalizer.

Santee turned and called out to the young woman who'd been bathing earlier. He peeled off his reeking frock coat and vest and threw them at her. "Wash those."

The girl wrinkled her nose and held the clothes at arm's length with a forefinger and thumb.

"Oooh, they stink," she said.

The deacon's anger flared. "Do as I say or I'll take a crop to you."

The girl sniffed and flounced toward the creek, still holding the deacon's coat and vest at arm's length.

He watched her go, grunted at Harcourt, then pulled his right-hand Smith & Wesson, broke it open, and punched out the spent shells. He reloaded with rounds from his pocket and did the same for his second revolver.

Santee holstered his guns and smiled at Harcourt. The rancher's handsome face creased as he returned the smile. It seemed that, despite everything, the deacon had forgiven him.

Santee drew and fired.

The bullet took off Harcourt's left thumb at the base, ranged downward after striking bone, and severed his forefinger at the second joint.

Harcourt screamed and clutched his wrist, staring in horror at his mutilated hand.

The deacon smiled. "That's your comeuppance

for deceiving me, Beau. For hiding my woman from me."

"You bastard!" Harcourt shrieked. "You piece of motherless scum."

Harcourt's right hand dropped to his gun, but the deacon's voice stopped him.

"I'll take the other one off at the wrist, Beau."

Harcourt very much wanted to live, an instinct stronger than his urge to kill.

He held his wrist again, his lips tight, grimacing against the pain.

Women tumbled out of the wagons and watched the scene in numb fascination. The cook and Harcourt's remaining puncher came running, then stopped when the deacon swung his icy eyes on them.

The puncher, a tall drink of water wearing batwing chaps and a worried expression, stepped beside Harcourt and said, "You all right, boss?"

Harcourt held up his bleeding hand. "What the hell do you think?"

The puncher glanced at Santee, looked away, and said, "How do I play this, Mr. Harcourt?"

"You don't, boy," the deacon said. "Not if you want to go on living."

The cowboy was young and there was a recklessness in him.

"You don't scare me none, mister," he said.

The almost benign expression on the deacon's face didn't change.

"I should," he said.

Harcourt kicked out at the puncher's leg. "Damn it, don't stand there trying to prove how brave you are. Tear up a shirt or something and bind my hand before I bleed to death."

The cowboy walked away and the deacon smiled. "I'd say that young man likes to live dangerously. What do you think, Beau?"

"Go to hell," Harcourt said, wincing against the pain.

"That won't happen, Beau. My destiny is to enter paradise and sit in a golden throne on the right hand of God. Such is the reward for piety and a life of prayer."

Chapter 30

Beau Harcourt sulked in his tent, drinking whiskey to dull the pain of the wound and the greater pain of his humiliation.

He'd folded after the deacon drew down on him. He hadn't even tried to make a play.

The raw whiskey burned Harcourt's throat. He watched a white moth flutter around the oil lamp, playing with fire.

His gun hand hadn't been injured.

Damn it, he should've tried.

Then he remembered.

"I'll take the other one off at the wrist, Beau."

Harcourt watched the moth and his eyes glazed. Growling like an animal, he tore the deacon apart, limb by limb . . . but only in his pain-tangled mind.

A vaquero rode into camp just before midnight.

Harcourt watched the Mexican trot to the deacon's wagons and step from the saddle.

Santee tumbled from the back of a wagon, yanking up his pants. An angry woman stuck her head out of the canvas and yelled something at him that Harcourt couldn't hear.

But she was mad as hell.

"The army wasn't at the river, señor," the vaquero said.

The deacon's anger flared. "What the hell do you mean?"

"No army. No money."

The man was silent for a while, then said, "Plenty of Apache sign in the hills, though. Maybe twenty, thirty bucks, no women or children."

"What do Gideon and Zedock say?"

The vaquero shrugged. "What the rest of us say, señor. The Apaches have broken out and the army is chasing them. They won't be buying beef anytime soon."

"Where is the herd?"

"On the Rio Puerco. The water is not good to drink and the graze is thin on both banks, señor.

If we don't move the herd soon, we'll have big losses."

"Harcourt's men still alive?"

The vaquero nodded. "*Sí, ellos todavia viven.*"

"Speak American, damn your papist eyes."

"They still live." Then he felt the need to explain. "A big fight over no money is a useless thing."

The deacon saw his thirty thousand dollars rapidly slip through his fingers.

Damn the Apaches and damn the damned army.

The Mexican pushed it as far as he dared. "*Patrón*, we must move the herd."

"Give me time to think, damn you," the deacon said.

South. He'd move south and take a chance that the Texas Rangers hadn't followed him this far.

"We'll bring the herd back here," he said. "We'll pick up Harcourt's thousand head and push south."

"To where?"

"Due south to Fort Apache. We need army money and that's where it's at."

The vaquero was appalled. "Señor, the fort is nearly thirty miles south of the Rim, across high country. We can't drive a herd due south over mountains."

"Then we'll keep to the valleys," the deacon said. "It'll only add five, six days to the drive if we push it."

"But many of the cows are already dying on their feet. We'll lose half of them."

"So? There will be enough of them left to make a profit. We take the money and keep on going into Old Mexico."

"The Apaches are out," the vaquero said. "We may have a big fight."

But the deacon was all through talking. "We'll do as I say. Do you hear me?"

He pulled the Mexican closer to him by his shirtfront. "Will you stick?"

The man nodded. "I ride for the brand, señor."

Deacon Santee smiled. "Good. Now listen well because we've got some killing to do."

Chapter 31

The wind had lain low all day, but now as night fell it gathered its strength and prowled restlessly around Requiem, its wandering path delineated by creaking timbers, the dry rustle of fallen leaves, and the *thud-thud* of unlatched doors.

Down by the graveyard the wild oaks tossed their branches and whispered ghostly stories to the attentive, bending pines.

The moon sailed high in the sky, scudding through billows of cloud, and small, timid things scurried among the buildings and added their hushed voices to the darkness.

Sam Pace stood at the window of his office and looked outside.

"A night for dead men to walk," he said.

Lake took a long time before he said anything, then said, "You goin' all loco on me again, boy?"

"I saw them, old man. Out there in the street."

"You saw them in a dream, Sam."

Without turning, Pace said, "Was it a dream? Or was I awake?"

"Dead men don't walk down Requiem's street."

"They do if they're hungry."

"Dead men don't get hungry. They don't get anything, except deader."

A quiet fell between the two men. Lake broke it.

"Sam, you don't go crazy in the head until you're back in this town," he said. "It's time you left and never came near the place again."

Pace turned and looked at the older man. "The people will return, Mash. They'll drive right down the street in wagons and after that, all the dead people will be gone."

Lake shook his head. "It's the town fer sure, making you crazy."

"You'll see," Pace said. "They'll come."

Lake had cleaned his and Pace's revolvers and now he began to reassemble the oiled parts lying on the desk in front of him.

He watched Pace lock the office door, then move to the window again.

The town was evil, Lake decided, or at the very least it exerted an evil spell over Sam Pace.

The younger man stared out into the street, expecing the dead to rise. Or was he watching for the return of the scattered citizens of Requiem?

Pace answered that question.

"I can feel something, Mash," he said. "The wind is telling me things."

"The only thing the wind is telling you, boy, is that you've gone crazy again."

Pace shook his head. "Can't you feel it? Smell it? The dead walking in the wind?"

Lake said nothing. He put the revolvers together, then reloaded the cylinders.

He held out Pace's Colt.

"Here, take this," he said. "If them dead folks come after you, you can hold 'em off for a spell."

Pace stepped to the desk, took the gun and dropped it into his holster. "You think I'm mad, don't you?"

"You are mad, son. As crazy as a loon. But only when you're in this damned town."

"The dead are about, Mash. I can tell they are."

The wind rose and the windows rattled in their frames.

Someone pounded on the door.

Pace's face froze and he backed away from the window, his hand on his gun.

"Damn it, boy," Lake said, pushing past him.

"Don't open it, Mash!"

Lake turned the key and grabbed the handle.

"No!" Pace drew his Colt.

The door swung open.

Jess fell into Lake's arms.

He half carried, half dragged her to the chair by the desk.

The woman's face was badly scraped by tree branches and she had a huge purple welt on the right side of her face. Her dress was torn and somewhere along the way she'd lost a shoe.

Pace had recovered from his fright.

"I'll get her something to eat," he said.

"Get the whiskey," Lake said. "Only danged fools like us eat peaches and bean stew."

Pace poured whiskey into a glass and Lake held it to Jess's mouth.

"Drink this," he said. "It will make you feel better."

The woman took a swallow and her eyes fluttered open.

"What damned fool locked the door?" she said. Her voice was weak, barely a whisper.

"Sam is the damned fool," Lake said. "He's afeared o' dead folks."

"Have you gone crazy again, Sammy?" Jess said.

"Yeah, seems like I'm tetched," Pace said.

"Then God help us all."

Lake moved to lay the glass on the desk, but the woman stopped him.

"Pour some more whiskey in there, Mash," she said. "And bring it back."

Pace built a cigarette and thumbed a match into flame. Through a spiral of blue smoke, he said, "Did Beau Harcourt do that to your face?"

"What do you think?"

"Was he trying to . . ." Pace couldn't find the words.

"Rape me?"

"Yes . . . that."

"He raped me." Jess's fingertips moved to the bruise. "He gave me this because he didn't enjoy it."

A quiet fell on the room as Pace and Lake fumbled for something comforting and reassuring to say. Women could have done it, but the men retreated into what they hoped was a sympathetic silence.

Jess smiled. "I'm a whore, remember? Every time a man pays me two dollars and throws himself on top of me, it's rape. You could say I'm used to it."

"More whiskey?" Pace said.

He couldn't think of anything else to say.

Chapter 32

Rain ticked on the roof and dripped from the eaves of the marshal's office. It was a light rain, but enough to lay the dust in the street for at least a while.

Jess stood at the window, her fingertip moving on a pane, tracing the descent of a raindrop.

"Why are we here?" she said.

Pace looked at Lake, who shrugged.

"Where?" Pace said.

"In Requiem."

"It's my town," Pace said.

"But it makes you mad."

"Maybe I feel safe here."

"You're not safe. The deacon, Beau Harcourt, the posse that's chasing after Mash, they all want us dead for one reason or another."

"That's no posse, girl," Lake said. "It's the four Peacock brothers. They ain't human, not by a long shot."

"The one who looked in the tent, was he one of them?"

"Yeah, he was a Peacock."

"He looked like death."

Lake smiled slightly. "He is death. All four of them are death."

Jess crossed the floor, took the burning cigarette from Pace's fingers, and inhaled deep. "We're living on borrowed time, but this doomed town keeps calling us back. It wants to keep us here, wants us to die here and join the others in the graveyard."

"Things will change," Pace said. "When the folks come back."

"Sammy, this is a ghost town," Jess said. "And you're a ghost marshal. Soon Requiem will crumble into dust and blow away in the wind."

She looked at Lake. "Mash, talk some sense into him."

The old man shook his head. "I've tried, and oncet or twicet I even thought he'd listened. But, like you said, as soon as he gets back in Requiem, he goes crazy again."

Lake laid a hand on Jess's shoulder.

"Sam can't leave Requiem because it's worked some kind of evil spell on him," he said. "I can't leave because the Peacocks will gun me for sure. But you can make a break for it, put some git between you and this place."

"You think so, Mash?"

"I'll bring a horse around front."

"No matter where I went, the deacon would hunt me down. He'll blame me for the deaths of his sons, just like he'll blame you two. I can't go far enough or fast enough to escape a man like that."

"There's the law. I mean, real law."

"Yes, Mash, you're right. But the law for whores isn't the same as the law for respectable folks." She shook her head. "No, I'm trapped, just like you" —she looked at Pace—"and the poor crazy man."

Jess glanced at the old railroad clock on the wall, its hand stilled at three twenty-seven.

"When did you last wind the clock, Sammy?" she said.

"I don't know," Pace said. "Three years ago, I guess."

"Then wind it and set the time by Mash's watch. It will measure the hours we have left, all of us."

The ticking railroad clock sounded like water dripping one drop at a time into a tin bucket. The oil lamp guttered in the wind, casting shifting shadows around the room, and the windows showed only darkness, as though the panes were covered with tarpaper on the outside.

The rain had stopped for now and no longer made its soft music.

Jess and Lake drowsed while Sam Pace worried.

The woman had been right about something. When he was in his office with the door closed, it felt as if he'd locked out the world and nothing could harm him.

He knew how wrong a thought that was.

Arrayed against him were some formidable enemies.

On his own, the deacon was a handful. Add his surviving sons and the border trash that rode for him, and it summed up to a dangerous combination.

Harcourt, a fast gun, had his punchers, all of them tough, hard-bitten men who would know how to fight.

And then there were the Peacock brothers.

But their fight was with Mash Lake, not himself.

Pace flushed at the traitorous thought.

Old Mash had laid his life on the line for him. To desert him now would be an unforgivable act of betrayal. He knew if he sold out Mash now, he could never again hold his head high in the company of men.

Ah well, the odds were insurmountable.

That's what it all boiled down to.

Pace glanced at the clock. Thirty minutes had passed since he'd gotten it running. Half an hour of his life already gone. How long did he have left?

He looked at Jess, then Lake. Suddenly they seemed vulnerable.

They depended on him, and he couldn't understand why.

No one should put their trust in a crazy man.

Pace rubbed a hand over his dry mouth, his blue eyes bleak.

The trouble was, in the scheme of things, none of it mattered.

The world didn't give a damn about the lives of a whore, a madman, and a creaky old-timer whose best days were long behind him.

If they all died today, tomorrow, the next day, who would care enough to mourn them?

Pace knew the answer to that question: not a living soul.

He sighed deep, shuddering, like an asthmatic trying to catch a breath.

He glanced at the clock on the wall, at the black hands of time that measured the hours of his life.

"Ah, the hell with it. Dying is easy," Pace said aloud. "It's the waiting that's hard."

The wolf howls woke Sam Pace from uneasy slumber.

He rose to his feet, stood, and listened into the night.

Had he been dreaming again, of wolves?

But once more the haunting howls ran through the darkness like rivers of quicksilver.

Alarmed, Pace shook Lake awake, nodded at Jess, and held a forefinger to his lips.

"Listen," he whispered.

As Pace had done, Lake stood, his face concerned.

The wolves howled and again the troubled night rang with their hollow cries.

Any man who's heard a pack hunt close and

says he was not afraid is a liar and he knows it. Only the mountains are unafraid of wolves. A man lies in his blankets, stares at the hunting moon, breathes quiet, and makes no sound, cursing the heart that beats so loud in his ears.

His own heart thudding like a drum, Pace led the way to the door and stepped outside. He and Lake walked into the street and their eyes immediately turned to the west where a fire burned.

The blaze was atop the rise on the outskirts of town, close enough for the two men to see eyes reflecting ruby red near its flames.

Four pairs of wolf eyes smoldered in the night . . . staring down at Pace. At Lake. At the town of Requiem.

"It's the Peacocks," Lake said. "They know I'm here."

"Wolves. Only wolves," Pace said.

"Wolves don't light fires."

Wolves don't light fires.

Pace drew his gun and motioned to Lake that he should do the same.

"Aim for the eyes," he said. "Empty your revolver at the sons of bitches."

"We can't hit nothin' at this range and in the dark."

"I know. But if it is the Peacocks, I want those boys to know that we ain't loafing around here, a-settin' on our gun hands."

Pace cut loose and Lake followed.

Instantly the fire was extinguished and the eyes vanished.

The racketing echoes of the gunshots died away . . . and once more an uneasy quiet descended on Requiem.

Chapter 33

"Is it done?" the deacon said, standing in darkness near his wagons.

The vaquero nodded. "*Sí*, señor. It is done."

The man's face was strained, and that troubled Santee.

"Cutting a man's throat bother you?" he said.

"Only the throat of the puncher. He lived in the saddle and nursed cows as I do. Now he is dead and I feel a little sad for him. As for the other one, it is no big thing to cut the throat of a cook."

"Our work isn't done yet," the deacon said. "There's one more."

"The man in the tent?"

"Yeah, him."

"He doesn't like vaqueros, calls us lazy greasers. Him, it will be a pleasure to kill."

"He's still got his gun hand and he's slick with the iron, so we'll step careful," the deacon said.

"I will get the job done, señor."

"No, we both will," Santee said.

He whispered something into the Mexican's ear that made the man grin.

The deacon slapped the vaquero on the shoulder. "All right, let's gun that son of a bitch."

"Wait," the vaquero said. "Do you hear it?" He hesitated, then said, "There it is again."

"Yeah. Sounds like wolves."

"I thought all the wolves were gone from this valley, many years ago."

"Maybe they're from up north, passing through to visit kin."

"It is strange, though," the vaquero said. "I mean, the wolves being here."

Irritated, the deacon stepped toward the tent.

"Let's go," he said. "I don't want to talk anymore about the damned wolves."

Harcourt's tent glowed dull orange in the darkness. The fading moonlight made the surrounding shadows deeper, darker—more ominous.

The deacon heard no sound from the herd. Around midnight he'd heard the cattle rise and graze for a few minutes before bedding down again.

With all his punchers out, the last thing he wanted was for the herd to run when he started shooting.

Unlike the longhorn scrubs he'd driven up the trail from Texas, Harcourt's cattle were white-faced shorthorns, placid creatures less inclined to stampede. But still, it was a worrisome thing.

He could use the knife on Harcourt, of course.

But Deacon Santee had never been much of a hand with the blade, though he'd cut uppity women a few times. Besides, the manner of Harcourt's impending death amused him.

He wouldn't miss it for the world.

On cat feet the deacon and the vaquero moved to the tent.

There was nothing to see from the front, so they moved to their right—and struck gold.

Harcourt sat on his cot, a dark silhouette against the background lamplight. His right arm moved occasionally, bringing a glass to his mouth.

The deacon smiled.

Lordy, Lordy, this was perfect.

He drew his guns and beside him the vaquero did the same. The young puncher grinned, enjoying this as much as his boss.

"Good evening, Beau," Santee said, quietly, like a man starting a conversation.

He fired as Harcourt jumped up from his cot.

Between them, the deacon and his vaquero pumped fifteen shots through the tent canvas. All but two of them hit their target.

Harcourt's body jerked like a rag doll as the heavy .45 balls tore into him, shredding his back and chest. Blood spattered the inside of the tent canvas as Harcourt's dying shrieks spiked into the night.

The deacon stepped out of a cloud of smoke and walked to the front of the tent.

He lifted the flap and looked inside, grinning.

Miraculously Harcourt was still alive. He lay on his back on the cot, his upper body drenched scarlet with blood. A bullet had torn away his lower jaw, and his eyes were wild.

Still grinning, the deacon took time to reload a revolver, then stepped beside the cot. He pushed the muzzle of the Smith & Wesson between Harcourt's terrified eyes.

"Nobody steals Deacon Santee's woman," he said.

He pulled the trigger.

The herd was restless, most of them standing, but they showed no inclination to run. Gradually the cattle calmed and began to graze and the deacon was pleased.

The shorthorns would put on beef for the drive south, and that was all to the good. He could count on fewer losses.

He reloaded both revolvers, deep in thought.

The bodies of the men he'd killed could remain where they lay. He'd send the vaquero to his sons and tell them to bring back the army herd for the trail south. They should arrive before noon and the dead men shouldn't be stinking too badly by then.

Except the cook.

Santee grinned. He'd gunned a trail cook once and the man had swelled up overnight and already stunk to high heaven come sunup, probably on account of him eating too much.

He nodded. It just went to show that moderation in all things was the key, something he himself practiced.

The deacon glanced toward the wagons. He had unfinished business with Maxine, or was it Leah? He couldn't remember. No matter, once the vaquero was gone he'd do both of them.

But then the damned Mex sidled up beside him and told Deacon Santee something that ruined his plans and his evening.

Chapter 34

"That's what I seen and I figured you should know," the vaquero said.

"Where the hell was this?" Santee said.

"About a mile north of the old ghost town."

"You saw them for sure?"

"With my own eyes."

"Why didn't you tell me before this?"

"I didn't think it so important."

"The buzzards could be circling my sons," the deacon said. "Did you think that wasn't important?"

The vaquero shrugged. "It is not likely. Señor Enoch is a pistolero and so is Jeptha. They would not fear the Apaches."

"Then why aren't they back here?"

The vaquero said nothing. The question was impossible to answer.

But the deacon pushed it. "Why aren't they here?"

"They toy with women, perhaps," the vaquero said, taking a stab at it.

"Maybe. Jeptha, my youngest, has a . . . fixation, I guess you'd call it . . . about blond women with bows in their hair."

"But just maybe he found one," the vaquero said. "Stranger things have happened."

"Yeah, maybe. Or an Apache bullet found him."

The deacon ordered the vaquero to mount up and tell Gideon and Zedock to return with the herd.

"I'll leave at first light and take a look for them buzzards you saw," he said. "If somebody killed my boys, Apache or white man, I'll tear this country apart until I find him."

"Maybe the killer, if such exists, lives in the ghost town," the vaquero said.

"Yeah, and that'll be the first damned place I'll look," the deacon said.

After the vaquero rode out, Santee stepped toward the wagons.

"Maxine!" he yelled. "You get ready."

He heard the woman give a pleasurable little squeal and it pleased him.

As he'd said so many times to his boys, all a man needed to break a woman was patience and a whip.

Just like a saddle mare.

Chapter 35

Jess Leslie crossed her hands and rubbed her upper arms, frowning.

"I feel dirty all over," she said. "I need to bathe."

"Stay clear of the well," Pace said. "Beau Harcourt's men stirred up the water and maybe they wakened the cholera."

"The creek?" Jess said.

"There's no cholera in the creek."

"Runs too fast, I reckon," Lake said.

"Then I'll bathe in the creek." She looked at the two men. "One of you will have to come with me. There's coyotes out there and maybe wolves and I don't want to be there alone."

Pace looked at Lake. "You, Mash?"

Lake shook his head. "No. I'm an old reprobate and I don't trust myself. I might take a peek."

"You won't see anything you haven't seen many times before," Jess said.

"I know, but nowadays my old heart wouldn't stand the excitement."

"Then it's you, Sammy," Jess said. "Let's go. If you think your heart can stand it."

"Kinda dark, isn't it?" Pace said.

"You protect me from the coyotes and I'll protect you from the boogerman," Jess said. "I don't want to feel soiled a moment longer than I have to."

She stepped to the door. "Are you coming?"

"Yeah, I guess so."

"Wouldn't do you any harm to take a bath yourself, sonny," Lake said.

"Sammy's a guard," Jess said. "He should keep his powder dry. Besides, I don't want him dirtying up my bathwater."

Pace was not in the best of moods as he picked up his rifle from the desk and followed the woman into the street.

As suddenly as it had begun, the wind had died. Now a gray haze hung over the town, and the blanched buildings looked like fading images on a tintype.

"Be fog come morning," Pace said. "Sometimes in summer it drifts up from the Mogollon Rim and covers the whole basin."

"If it wasn't so scary, it would be pretty," Jess said.

Pace smiled. "Now who's sceered of the boogerman?"

• • •

Jess chose a spot where the creek flowed between two rocks, creating a sieve of white water about three feet deep.

She stripped in the waning moonlight and her slender naked body was as pale as bone.

Pace had taken himself off a ways and fetched his back against the trunk of a cottonwood, the Winchester between his drawn-up knees.

It had been three years since he'd seen a naked woman, and he watched Jess with pleasure, but without desire, as a man looks at a nude painting in an art gallery.

Jess stood in the water, then lowered herself into the eddies. She squealed as the sting of the icy creek hit her butt, and then kneeled without moving for long moments, letting her body get accustomed to the cold.

Pace smiled, enjoying himself.

But, when the woman began to wash her shadowed, secret places, he turned away to spare her shame.

The creek flowed through a series of shallow rock shelves. The upper levels ran over a clay bed, the lower over pebbles.

The fog, spreading, was now drifting into the higher shelves and between the trunks of the cottonwoods and pines growing on the banks.

Jess was now a white blur in the misty gloom, but Pace heard her splash water. And, God help her, he thought, she was actually humming a little tune.

Pace shook his head in admiration.

The girl looked fragile, frail as a china doll, but, mentally and physically, she was enduring, as strong as any man, himself included.

His wife had been like that, the perfect spouse for a lawman.

Then she was taken by the cholera and all that had been wonderful in her came to an end, leaving a vast emptiness in Pace that nothing could ever fill.

Pace heard Jess get out of the water and he stepped toward her.

She stood on the bank shivering, and then began to pick up her clothes.

"You can't dress without getting dry first," Pace said.

"I don't have a towel, Sammy. Didn't you notice?"

The woman's nakedness didn't trouble Pace, nor did it her.

"Damn it, here." Pace slipped the canvas suspenders from his shoulders and took off his shirt. "Use this," he said. "It's clean, or fairly clean."

"You'll be cold," Jess said.

"I'll be just fine."

He held up the shirt. "Now put it on. It will dry you and keep you warm."

There's no accounting for what a woman will and will not do, but Jess smiled and did as Pace told her.

She was closing the last shirt button when the wolves howled again.

Close this time. Very close.

Chapter 36

Sam Pace racked a round into the chamber of his rifle as his eyes scanned the opposite creek bank where pine tops lifted like obsidian arrowheads into the sky, their trunks lost in mist.

The wolves howled again and Pace felt fear clutch at him.

"Get back to town," he whispered to Jess. "Tell Mash."

The woman clutched her clothes to her breast, her face drained of color. "Come with me, Sammy. The wolves will kill you."

"They're human wolves," Pace said. "It's the Peacock brothers. They'd cut us down in the street before we reached my office."

He turned his head, and, his voice urgent, he said, "Jess, you git now."

The woman needed no second bidding. She fled into the night, wolf howls following her.

Pace took cover behind the cottonwood, watching, waiting.

A few moments of sullen silence slunk past, slow enough that Pace had time to dry his fear-sweated hands on his pants and clutch his rifle again.

A bullet *thunk*ed into the tree trunk and another chipped bark near Pace's face, driving splinters into his cheek.

Damn it, them Peacock boys could see in the dark.

A voice rose from the gray and black gloom, hollow and echoing, like a man speaking in a sepulcher.

"Mash Lake, is that you? Step out and take your medicine."

Pace thought he had a fix on the location of the speaker, but he wasn't sure. He needed the man to speak again.

"This is Lake," he said. "State your business."

He lifted the Winchester to his shoulder.

"You know our business," the man yelled. "You killed our brother. There is talking to be done, a reckoning to be made."

Pace aimed into darkness. Now he knew the spot among the trees where the Peacocks were hidden.

His finger took up a quarter inch of slack on the trigger.

"Come out, Lake. We want to—"

Pace fired.

He levered shells into the Winchester and dusted shots to the right and left of the speaker's location.

Suddenly a man yelped like a wounded cur . . . and kept on yelping, each shriek rising to a higher pitch.

A rifle blasted beside Pace and Lake threw himself to the ground.

"Is it the Peacocks?" he said.

"Yeah, and I winged one of them."

"I heard him squeal."

Lake fired in the direction of the yelps, and Pace's rifle joined in the fusillade.

They shot their rifles dry but there was no return fire.

Gun smoke drifted and became one with the gray mist.

"They quit," Pace said. "Damn it, they just gave up and left."

"They haven't left," Lake said. "The Peacock boys are sure-thing killers and they didn't like this ground, was all. They'll be back."

"The question is, when?" Pace said.

"The answer is, when it gets light. They know we're holed up in the ghost town and that's where they'll come lookin'."

"I think we can take them, Mash," Pace said. "They didn't seem so all-fired tough tonight."

"Maybe. So we burned them. All that means

is they'll be more careful next time. I told you afore, Sam, we can't shade them boys in a close-up gunfight."

"Then we won't let them get close."

Lake nodded. "I got an idea on that score, but we won't be fightin'. We'll be hidin'."

"Until they give up and go away?"

"That's the plan."

"Sounds thin, Mash."

"Hell, boy, it is thin. But is all I've got. You?"

"A long-range rifle fight, I reckon. Out in the hills, maybe."

"Try that and you'll be dead," Lake said. "From now on the Peacocks will be prepared and they'll get close, revolver close. We got lucky tonight. We won't get lucky a second time."

"You sure know how to cheer a man, don't you?" Pace said, turning his head to regard the old man.

"Yep. I do it all the time. You might say that it's my nat'ral sunny disposition."

Chapter 37

"I'm your prisoner, Sammy," Jess said. "I have to go where you go."

"That doesn't signify any longer," Pace said.

"Changed your mind, huh?"

"Yes, I have. I made you my prisoner when I was tetched. I'm not tetched anymore."

"Could've fooled me, Sam," Lake said. "The way you was talking about bracing them Peacock brothers."

"I may still brace them, Mash. There was a time I was considered a man who was pretty good with a gun."

"Pretty good don't cut it, Sam, not with the Peacocks."

"Hell, Mash, we sent 'em running. How good can they be?"

"They're revolver fighters, Sam. A gunfight in darkness and fog isn't their thing, if'n you get my meaning."

"Then why the hell did they shoot?"

"Because they thought you were me. They expected a feeble old man who'd get scared and try to talk them out of it." Lake smiled.

"Instead they bumped into a feller who was once considered pretty good with a gun."

Jess handed Pace his damp shirt. "Dry that in front of the stove," she said.

She laid a hand on Pace's shoulder. "So, how come you aren't crazy no more, Sammy?"

"Because I suddenly realize that I'm the marshal of nothing." He reached into his pocket, found his star, and threw it on the desk. "I've been fooling myself. The people aren't coming back, not to this bad-luck ghost town, they aren't."

"And the dead people down at the graveyard who want to eat you for supper?" Jess said.

Pace hesitated. "I don't know about them. At least, not yet."

Lake smiled his approval at Jess. "Good, now it seems ol' Sam is only half crazy."

"The church bell tower has been rotting away for three years," Pace said. "It may not be safe any longer, if it ever was."

"It only needs to hold us until the Peacock brothers give up and leave," Lake said.

"If they decide to search the church, we'll be trapped like rats," Pace said.

"That's a chance we'll have to take. I reckon they'll ride through, like, and then figure we lit out for the hills."

Pace looked at Jess. "What do you think?"

The woman was quiet for a few moments, wrinkles gathering between her eyebrows.

Finally she said, "We can't run and let them catch us in the open, so we're stuck here. And it's not just the Peacocks. You killed two of the deacon's sons, and he'll come after you. It's only a matter of when and he'll pick a time that suits him."

She took the shirt from Pace's hands and spread it over the stove. "The bell tower is as good a place as any to hide. At least up there, we'll be closer to our Maker."

Pace talked through a sigh. "Well, I guess that's it. We'll hide in the tower and hope"—he slammed a hand on the desk—"hell no, we'll not. If the Peacock boys discover we're up there, they can stand off and shoot the tower to pieces and us with it."

"So, what does the genius suggest?" Jess said.

"We mount up and make a run for it. In open country Mash and me can keep the Peacocks at rifle distance. There's a Mormon settlement west of Silver Creek by the name of Snowflake and we can head for there. They'll have law and fighting men enough to enforce it."

"And the deacon?" Jess said.

"I don't think we have anything to fear from him, at least for a spell," Pace said. "He's got important business with Beau Harcourt and that will occupy him."

Lake looked at the woman. "Jess?"

"I still think hiding out is the best idea, but I'll go along for the ride," she said.

"That only leaves you, Mash," Pace said.

"Hell, Sam, I ain't staying here by my own self with the Peacocks and the deacon and the hungry dead people and the hants an' sich. I'll play it your way."

Lake rose to his feet and stepped toward the door.

"You two pack up as much grub as you can find," he said. "I'll get the horses."

After Lake left, Pace stood at the window and looked outside.

The night was shading into dawn, but the fog was so thick he couldn't see a thing beyond the boardwalk. There was no wind to stir the mist and it hung like a damp gray blanket over the town.

Jess had filled a burlap sack with canned food. Now her eyes moved to the window and she too let her gaze search into the fog.

"Can we find our way in this?" she said.

"We'll leave it to the horses to pick a trail," Pace said. "Anyway, the same fog that slows us will slow the Peacocks."

"Mash says they're half wolf."

"They're men, like any other men. I proved that when I shot one of them at the creek."

Jess was silent for a while, then said, "Sammy,

I don't think you shot one of the brothers. I don't think you shot anybody."

"What do you mean?"

"A shot man doesn't shriek like that . . . like an animal. They want you to think that one of them is down so you'll lower your guard just a little. Professional gunmen like the Peacock brothers will always look for an edge, no matter how slight."

Pace thought for a few moments. He said, "I reckon it troubled me at the time. I mean, that they gave up so fast. I couldn't quite figure that one out."

"As Mash says, it wasn't their kind of gunfight and you weren't the one they were after. They did their wounded wolf cry and backed away from it."

"To fight another day when the circumstances will be more in their favor."

"Right. When they have an edge."

Pace nodded. "They won't have an edge out in the open country. I'll see to that."

But Pace was talking into the wind.

There would be no open country.

Mash Lake stepped into the marshal's office, his face a stony mask.

"We ain't going anywhere," he said.

"Why the hell not?" Pace said.

"Because the horses are gone."

Chapter 38

"What do you mean the horses are gone?" Sam Pace demanded.

Lake's voice revealed his irritation.

"How many ways do you want me to say it, Sam? The horses are gone. Departed, skedaddled, vanished, vamoosed."

"Mash," Jess said, "did the Peacocks take them?

Lake shook his head. "It was Apaches. Lifted them horses as nice as you please in the fog."

"Are you sure?" Pace said.

"Sure of what, Sam? That the horses are gone?"

Annoyed, Pace said, "Hell no. I mean that they were stolen by Apaches."

"Moccasin sign all over the place. Judging by the tracks, I'd say White Mountain, but I could be wrong."

His anger growing, Pace said, "An Apache is an Apache. Don't make a hill o' beans difference what kind he is."

"Maybe you're right, Sam," Lake said. "When a man's got his feet to the fire, it don't matter a damn what kind of Injun's holding on to his ankles."

The three fell silent, Pace and Jess having it in

their heads that Lake's news had brought them no pleasure and considerable worry.

"Will they attack us, Mash?" Jess said finally.

"Apaches are notional," Lake said. "You can never tell what they'll do from one minute to the next. But I reckon this was a horse raid and they ain't lookin' fer a fight, at least not yet and not with us."

"The army?" Jess said.

"Seems likely enough. They've broken out, and they know the horse so'jers will be after them."

Jess looked at Pace. "Well?"

"Well what?"

"Well, what do we do now, Sammy? Hoof it?"

"We won't get far on foot. The Peacocks will ride us down and hit us when we least expect it."

"And the Apaches are painted for war," Lake said. "Another mighty good reason for staying right where we're at."

"You talking about that damned bell tower again?" Pace said.

"Unless you can think of a better place," Lake said.

"I'm studying on it."

"Don't study on it too long, Sam. We're within spittin' distance of death right now."

"The graveyard," Pace said, as though he'd had a sudden burst of intuition. "Apaches won't go near a place where folks are buried."

"Maybe, maybe not," Lake said. "But the Peacocks will."

"All right, then, we could just head out of town, hole up in the hills someplace," Pace said.

"If the Apaches are around, they'd find us fer sure," Lake said.

"Oh, for God's sake, you two!" Jess said, her cheekbones flaring red. "The Apaches, the Peacocks, the deacon—they'll all be here sooner than you think. We'll hide in the bell tower. It's our only chance."

"Like rats," Pace said.

"Live rats," Jess said.

"The lady makes sense, Sam," Lake said. "I think we've fresh run out of options."

"Damn the Apaches, and damn this bad-luck town," Pace said.

"Now you sound almost sane, boy," Lake said. "And that's surely an encouragement to all of us."

The church had been a hurried afterthought by a few of the more pious residents of Requiem, but it had still not attracted a preacher before the cholera epidemic hit.

It was a rickety timber structure, shoddily and quickly built as the town sought instant respectability.

During its twelve months of existence, it had been pushed into service as a dance hall, a storage place for winter ice and beer barrels, and latterly a makeshift morgue for the cholera dead.

The top of the bell tower was accessed by a ladder that ascended to an open rectangle about four feet wide on all sides. Much of the space was taken up by a rusty iron bell that hung from an oak beam, and a wooden railing, as high as a man's waist, enclosed the area.

The tower was cramped, smelled of rotten wood, and was known to sway alarmingly in a high wind, but on a clear day it gave a good view of the town and the surrounding area.

But all Pace could see as he moodily stared into the distance was a gray lake of fog that stretched in all directions.

"Make yourselves comfortable," he said. "We could be here for quite a spell."

Lake sounded grumpy. "Hey, suppose I have to take a piss?"

"Over the side, Mash," Jess said.

"And what about you?" Lake said.

"Over the side."

"Hell, I'd like to see that."

"If we're here long enough, you will," Jess said.

"We don't have enough water stored up here for that to be a problem," Pace said.

Chapter 39

Deacon Santee was lost in the fog, and that annoyed the hell out of him.

But worse, he'd seen the tracks of shod and unshod horses all heading west and that could only mean raiding Apaches making off with their plunder.

His herd and wagons were in that direction. The women he could replace, but the cattle and wagons were too valuable to be taken by thieving Indians.

The deacon was worried. If he didn't find the damned ghost town soon, he might be forced to return to camp to protect his property.

He had prayed for God to show him the way of course, but the deity must have been preoccupied with weightier matters elsewhere because he was even more lost now than he'd been before.

He led his horse through a thicket of oak and pine, wading into mist so thick he couldn't see his hand in front of his face.

The sun was up, but did nothing to penetrate the tree canopy, and he stumbled around like a man in a pitch-dark room.

Santee stopped and lit a cigar and stood thinking.

He must be close to the ghost town.

The vaquero had given him directions, but neither of them had accounted for fog. He felt like a lost soul condemned to wander forever in a milk-white hell.

Then he caught the stink.

The rotting dead smell sweet, a cloying stench that immediately assaults the nose and curdles the stomach. It stays with a man. If he comes across a corrupting body before breakfast, its sickening rankness will be his companion at supper.

And a horse is no friend to the dead.

The deacon's mount tried to back away. It tugged on the reins, head high, white arcs of fright in its eyes.

Santee cursed the animal and dragged it forward through the murk.

He followed his nose.

The corpses lay together, faces blue, postmortem gasses swelling bellies tight against their shirts, threatening to burst and hiss vile foulness into the fog.

The faces of Enoch and Jeptha were almost unrecognizable, but Deacon Santee knew his own.

He did not kneel, or pray (he reserved his prayers only for himself), but he threw back his head and shrieked his anger at a trembling heaven.

He called curses down on the one who had murdered his sons. He demanded of the vengeful God of his own creation that the man's get be damned until the end of time, seed, breed, and generation.

Even in his more placid moments, Deacon Santee was a cold-blooded, vicious killer. Now, in his blind rage, he was dangerous beyond all measure.

He raised his hands above his head in supplication and demanded that the fog lift.

"There is killing to be done," he yelled, cigar clamped between his teeth. "All the powers of heaven and hell, disperse ye now this damnable mist."

The deacon removed his top hat and fetched his back against a tree.

The stench of death in his nostrils . . . he waited.

An hour later, the fog began to lift and gaps appeared in the solid grayness like rips in a curtain.

Below Santee, deep in a shelving valley, the curtain finally parted, revealing a town.

The deacon swung into the saddle and rode down the rise, bringing hell with him.

Chapter 40

After the fog hitched up its skirts and fled, the sun rose in the sky and laid a heavy hand on the wide land.

The day was hot, without a breath of wind, and the deacon sweated under his heavy broadcloth.

He dismounted at the far end of town, tied his horse to the hitch rail outside a barbershop, and looked around.

A single row of gray-faced stores, most of them with false fronts, led the way toward a ramshackle church that had seen better days, a sight that made the deacon cluck in disapproval.

The least the folks here should've done before they left was to tear it down. That would've been right and proper. It was a grievous sin to let a house of worship rot in the sun like an unwanted corpse.

Before he left he would set the church on fire and let it be consumed by purifying flames.

After a last glance at the church, the deacon drew his guns and stepped into the barbershop.

Thick dust lay everywhere, cobwebs triangled the corners and a pack rat had built its untidy nest on the seat of the chair. A bench placed against the wall was littered with sheets of yellowed newspaper, and unswept clippings of hair still covered the floor.

Santee strolled to a shelf behind the chair, picked up a dark blue bottle, and dusted it off. Lavender water. His favorite. He pulled the cork, sniffed to make sure the scent was still potent, then took off his top hat and poured the stuff over his bald head.

He nodded his approval, then tossed the empty bottle through the shop window. As shattered glass chimed around him, he smiled.

A man should smell good.

The heat of the day slamming him, the deacon began a systematic search of the town buildings. He found an unopened bottle of bourbon in the saloon, drank deeply, then carried it with him during the rest of his search.

A gun in one hand, the bottle in the other, Santee reached the marshal's office.

He was sweating like a pig and his skin itched. He decided this was the hottest day of the summer so far, what they called a "scorcher" back east, and the bourbon was making him thirsty.

He threw away the half-empty bottle and then kicked in the door of the marshal's office.

His gun up and ready in front of him, he followed the revolver inside, then stopped in his tracks.

Someone had been there—and recently.

And he smelled a woman.

Jessamine! It had to be. She had been here and not so long ago.

There were three cups on the table, evidence of meals, cigarette butts, and the coffeepot was still warm. The railroad clock on the wall was ticking, so it had been wound recently.

The room told its story to Santee.

After fleeing Harcourt his woman had found refuge here, and her companions were probably male. Two of them. They could be the sons of bitches who had murdered his sons.

The deacon checked the cell at the rear of the office, found nothing of interest, and stepped back into the street.

He still had a few other buildings to search, including the church. If he found no trace of Jess and the men with her, he'd scout the brush and mesquite country around the town.

Damn it, they were here recently and they must be close.

But where?

The hammering sun used Requiem as an anvil, beating the town into fiery submission. Such breeze as there was felt like a draft from a blast furnace and the air was thick and hard to breathe.

As the deacon paced down the middle of the street, a dust devil spun around his feet and lifted the tails of his frock coat. He stumbled, and then walked on. The devil spun behind him, then collapsed in a puff of dust.

Santee reached into a pocket of his frock coat, found a large red bandanna, and mopped sweat from his head and face. He squinted against the glare of the sun and rubbed the back of his hand across his mouth, tasting salt.

Just ahead of him was a well, hopefully still with water, and he walked toward it.

Above him, buzzards flew lazy triangles in the sky and the hazed sun smoked like a white-hot coin. Sunlight reflected from store windows, adding more heat to the blazing day, and nothing moved or made a sound. Even the crickets had quit fiddling.

The deacon removed his coat, folded it neatly, and laid it on the ground beside the well. He unbuckled his guns and placed them on top of the coat.

A wooden bucket had been untied from the pulley rope and thrown aside. Santee reattached the bucket and lowered it into the well. He was gratified to hear a splash when it hit bottom.

He waited, then worked the pulley handle. The bucket reappeared, crystal-clear water cascading over its rim.

A rusty dipper lay nearby on the well's limestone wall. The deacon wiped it off with his fingers, filled the dipper from the bucket, and drank deeply.

The water was cool and sweet and he refilled the dipper and drank again.

Deacon Santee had no way of knowing that he'd just tasted death a second time.

Chapter 41

"The deacon is drinking from the well," Sam Pace said.

"Will it kill him?" Jess said.

Pace kept his eye to the railing, staring through a chink between a pair of warped boards.

"I don't know." He turned and smiled at Jess. "You sound hopeful."

"I am," the woman said. "Hell, how long does the cholera poison a well? Months? Years?"

"I don't know that either. But Harcourt's boys stirred the water up when they gave me a bath. If there's still cholera in the well, I'd say they wakened it up for sure."

"How does it kill a man?" Lake said.

"If he's took sick in the morning, most times he'll be dead by sundown."

"If the deacon did drink poisoned water, how long before he gets sick?" Jess said.

"It's mighty sudden. Three, maybe four hours."

"Then what happens, Sammy?"

"Everything that's inside you comes out both ends," Pace said, "and it keeps on a-coming. Your legs cramp up and you can't walk and you get a raging fever. If you have the strength, you'll scream for a while, but pretty soon you die." He smiled. "One of the good Lord's tender mercies."

"I wouldn't wish a death like that on anyone," Lake said. He looked at Pace. "My God, Sam, you saw a whole town die like that, including your own wife and wee babby? How could you stand it?"

Pace said nothing, his eyes unfocused, looking back into a different place and time.

"No wonder you're tetched in the head, boy," Lake said finally, a sense of wonder in his voice.

"Sammy," Jess said, "your wife. Was she pretty?"

It was a female question and Pace accepted it with a tolerant smile.

"Yes, very pretty. She had . . . she had this yellow hair and the sun would get all tangled in it and turn it gold. And she had gray eyes, like a summer mist, only sometimes they looked blue." His head turned to the side as he remembered. "In the dark, or by lamplight, that's when they were blue. Dark, kinda like the night sky."

"You loved her very much, didn't you, Sammy?" Jess said.

"Yeah. I did. I loved her very much. I still do."

"I didn't want to drive you crazy again, Sammy," Jess said.

"You didn't. The death of his wife leaves a heartache in a man that no one can heal." Pace smiled. "But the way he loved her, well, that's a memory no one can ever steal from him."

"Will you ever be able to love another woman?" Jess said.

Pace grinned, his teeth white under his mustache. "Are you volunteering, Jess?"

"Men don't fall in love with whores, Sammy," Jess said.

"You're not a whore now," Pace said.

Lake coughed. "What's the deacon doing now, Sam?" he said.

Pace left the place where he'd been and returned to the present. "Still drinking. He must have a powerful thirst."

"Hell, so do I," Lake said. "But not for that well water."

"You can drink from the canteen soon, Mash. I don't want you filling up with water, then pissing all over the place like you said you would."

The bell tower was open to the sun, and the small platform built up heat. Pace and the others were soaked with sweat, and even the slightest movement became an intolerable chore.

Jess moved slightly, and the back of her neck brushed the iron bell. She yelped and jerked away.

"The bell's red-hot," she said.

"Did the deacon hear that yip, Sam?" Lake asked, alarmed. "Is he looking this way?"

"I don't think so," Pace said. "He doesn't seem to be interested in the tower."

He turned to Jess. "Don't do that again."

"Do you think I did it on purpose, Sammy?"

"No, I don't. But don't do it again just the same."

"Now what's he doin'?" Lake said.

"Nothing. Just standing there."

"He's got to be doin' something."

"Nope, he's just standing there."

Pace's shoulders stiffened. "Wait. He's buckling on his guns. Now he's putting on his hat. Now his frock coat. He's tying a wet bandanna around his neck."

"Hell," Jess said, "this is exciting stuff."

"Now what?" Lake said.

Pace rubbed his eyes. "I reckon the only place he's got left to search in Requiem is the church. He'll probably head straight for here."

"And that's right where we're at," Lake said.

"I'm glad you told us, Mash," Jess said. "We wouldn't have known."

The oldster smiled. "Young lady, someday I'll put you over my knee and tan the seat of your britches with a willow switch."

"Bring an army with you, Mash Lake. You'll need it."

"Hey, quit bickering, you two," Pace said. "Something's happening."

"What's he doin', Sam? Coming our way?" Lake said.

"No. He's staring at something."

"Where?"

"To the east of town."

"What's he see?" Lake said.

"Hell, I don't know what he sees."

But then Pace did know.

And with that knowledge death brushed past him like a cold breeze.

Chapter 42

"Well, now," the deacon said aloud to himself, as was his habit. "What the hell have we here?"

Four riders came down off the ridge and onto the flat.

For a few moments the shimmering heat haze elongated both men and horses so they looked gaunt, emaciated, like the Four Horsemen of the Apocalypse in a stained glass window.

The Peacock brothers rode closer, resumed their mortal size, and headed in the deacon's direction.

Santee, a careful man, drew his revolvers and set them on the flat parapet of the well.

When the riders were close enough, he smiled and said, "Howdy, boys. Good to see you again. You catch up with that feller you was hunting?"

The younger Peacock's mouth moved, no sound coming out.

"Is the water good to drink?" his brother said for him.

The deacon nodded. "It's cool and sweet. He'p yourself, boys."

The young Peacock's mouth moved again, his blue, staring eyes fixed on the deacon.

His brother said, "We know where the man called Mash Lake is. He is here, in this place, and here we will destroy him."

"Beggin' your pardon, boys, but where?" Santee said. "I've been all over the damned town." He holstered his guns, a movement that tensed the Peacocks. "I reckon he's one of the murdering scum who killed my sons."

The dumb Peacock spoke again without words.

"There are three of them," his brother said for him. "Two men and a woman."

"Where?"

"In the church bell tower."

"Hell, how do you know that? I ain't seen nobody. Of course, I haven't searched the church yet."

The wordless Peacock's lips moved.

"Nonetheless, that is where they are," his brother said, his words exactly matching the lip movements. "I can smell their sweat and their fear."

"Then let's go get them," the deacon said.

The Peacocks didn't react to Santee's suggestion.

They dismounted and passed around the dipper

and, like the deacon, drank deeply, for the day was hot and the air as dry as bone.

"Did you see coal oil in any of the stores?" one of the brothers asked.

"Yes, I think I did." The deacon turned and pointed. "Over there, to the general store."

"Then we will use it," the silent Peacock said.

Talking to a mute who could only speak through his brother spooked Santee, and if there weren't four of the Peacocks he would have shot the dumb son of a bitch for the sake of his own peace of mind.

One of the brothers who hadn't spoken before said, "Gather up the coal oil and bring it to the saloon."

He said this to the deacon, who immediately took offense. He wasn't a lackey to be bossed around like a common laborer.

Then he looked at the man's face.

Like his brothers', his skin was drawn tight to the skull, fish-belly white, thin lips of the same shade. But his eyes burned with an unholy green fire, unblinking, measuring, relentless.

The deacon looked away. *Damn it, you're not a man. You're a demon.*

"I'll bring the coal oil right away," the deacon said.

Santee stepped out of the saloon and glanced at the bell tower. There was no sign of life.

180

Nothing moved and there was no sound. Dead quiet.

He shook his head.

Hell, if the Peacocks claimed they were up there, then they were up there.

Them boys seemed to know things mortal folks didn't.

It was downright strange.

"We'll light the fire at dusk," one of the brothers said. "We wish to watch the flames light Mash Lake's path to hell."

Deacon Santee had given up trying to tell the Peacocks apart. He filled their glasses from a dusty bottle of Hennessy cognac he'd found under the bar counter.

"Drink hearty, one and all," he said. He raised his glass. "Here's to the darkness and the flames."

The brothers ignored him.

The mute's mouth moved and his brother filled in the words.

"Here's some fun. Who among us will toll the bell? Come, now, we need a volunteer."

"You mean fer them in the tower?" the deacon said.

Another brother grinned and looked at Santee, his teeth large and yellow in his mouth.

" 'Never send to know for whom the bell tolls. It tolls for thee,' " he said.

"Ah yes," the deacon said, "that's in the Good Book, ain't it?"

"The English poet John Donne wrote that line three hundred years ago."

"That was gonna be my second guess," the deacon said, blinking.

"Come, now, who will toll the bell?" the speechless Peacock said, his silent mouth smiling as his brother spoke for him. "Let's have some fun."

Four pairs of green eyes focused on Santee.

The deacon forced a smile. "It will be my pleasure," he said. "I'll take pots at it with a rifle, right?"

"No, you will toll the bell," the mute said. "With the rope. There's good sport for all and no mistake."

The deacon met the man's eyes and quickly glanced away.

Damn, it was like staring into green ice and hellfire.

He felt a niggling little twinge of pain in his belly.

Was it caused by fear of the Peacocks or the damned brandy?

He didn't know.

But he did know enough to say "I'll haul on the rope. Wake them up, huh?"

"Yes, haul on the rope," a brother said. "We knew you would."

Chapter 43

Apart from a few scattered gingerbread houses, cactus growing in yards that once boasted flowers and grass, the church was isolated at the east end of town.

The deacon looped to the north, then east, slipping through trees and brush as slick and silent as an Apache. By the time he came up on the rear of the church, he figured he hadn't been seen.

He became certain of that last when he spotted the Peacocks standing on the boardwalk outside the saloon, brandy glasses in hand, their amused eyes fixed on the belfry of the bell tower.

Santee figured that if there were folks in the tower like the dummy said, they'd be watching the brothers just as closely.

A door at the rear of the church stood ajar, angled outward on just its bottom iron hinge.

The deacon drew his gun and, avoiding a clump of cactus in the doorway, stepped through.

Years before, the church pews had been cleared from the floor and stacked against the walls to make room for dancing. Bats hung from the roof beams and added their fetid smell to the odors of dry rot and decay. The oak pulpit had pulled away from its supports and crashed to the floor, where its panels had blossomed open like a dropped barrel.

The church that had never been a house of worship was rotting inside and out, and it was tinder dry.

The deacon studied the place, his nose wrinkling.

Coal oil be damned. He reckoned he could set the whole shebang ablaze with a single match.

He crossed the limestone floor, quick on his feet. His frock coat flapped around his skinny legs, giving him the look of a tiptoeing crow.

Then he stopped dead in his tracks and doubled over. He felt as though somebody had just rammed a rifle butt into his belly.

The deacon grimaced as he clenched back a knifing spasm of pain in his gut.

Suddenly he felt hot and unwell.

Was he "coming down with something," as his wives always said?

It had to be the brandy. The bottle had sat in the saloon for years collecting dust and had probably gone bad.

Yeah, that made sense.

He just hoped the damned rotgut was hurting the Peacocks as much as it was him.

It took a minute or so before the deacon felt well enough to pass through the shattered doorway that led to the vestibule.

He looked around, his gun up and ready.

The baptistery lay to his left, and to the right of the main entrance was another doorway that must lead to the bell tower.

Unlike the other doors in the church, this one was intact, its timber panels as solid as the day it was built. Only the tarnished brass handle showed age.

Santee opened the door and walked into a small, rectangular room.

A ladder led upward into the belfry and ended at a closed trapdoor. The bell rope hung almost to the floor, knotted at the end for the convenience of a reverend who had never rung it.

The deacon stepped to the ladder, and then he doubled over as pain stabbed at him. It was a brief, intense spasm that finally passed as the others had done before. But he felt that his bowels were loosening and that worried him.

For a brief moment, he leaned his forehead against the ladder, willing his churning belly to settle. A wave of nausea swept over him and he broke out in a clammy sweat, biting back the urge to vomit all over the floor.

The deacon groaned. What the hell was happening to him?

Too much brandy and too much sun had done for him.

It was as simple as that.

Finally he gathered his strength, grabbed the ladder, and lifted it away from the trapdoor. He angled the ladder against the far wall, well out of reach of the fugitives.

Despite his growing weakness and the green sickness curling in his gut, the deacon managed a smile.

Now that vile whore Jessamine and her protectors were well and truly trapped.

Like rats in a cage.

The deacon stepped to the bell rope and grabbed it with both hands. He cocked his head to one side, listening.

There was no sound.

Up there, above him, they were being as quiet as cowering little mice, afraid of being discovered.

The irony of that pleased the deacon. Soon there would be plenty of noise—when the bell started clanging.

He clutched at his belly and bent over as another spasm slammed at him. This time he threw up, foul-smelling water and booze mixed with green bile splashing at his feet.

After a while, when the final dry heaves ended, he straightened and wiped off his mouth with the back of his hand. He was trembling, sweat beading on his forehead.

He was sick, very sick, as sick as a pig, and he didn't know why.

Had the Peacocks slipped poison into his brandy?

He dismissed that possibility as soon as he thought about it. If the Peacocks wanted him dead, they would've shot him.

Poison wasn't their style.

Too much brandy, then. And he'd drunk whiskey beforehand.

There is a serpent in every bottle and he biteth like the viper.

He had overindulged, was all, a mistake the deacon vowed never to make ever again.

As long as he lived.

He took a deep breath, grabbed the rope, and yanked hard.

The bell clamored, clanged, its clashing iron reverberating through the church, a shrill, ear-shattering cacophony that sent the bats shrieking from their roosts.

The deacon screamed laughter, pumping on the rope, his coat flapping behind him like the tail feathers of a bedraggled rooster.

Even when his bowels finally gave way, he went right on screeching.

"Wake up, little mice! It's time for church!"

Chapter 44

Sam Pace was drowsing when the bell jangled him awake.

"What the hell?" he yelled, springing to his feet.

Jess and Lake had covered their ears, their faces screwed up in pain.

The bell swung back and forth, the clapper clamoring like a tongue in an iron mouth.

Pace threw himself on the bell and circled it with his arms. The hot metal scorched his hands, but he held it still and the sound stilled to a ringing silence.

The rope jerked, jerked again. Pace left the bell alone and grabbed the rope. He pulled, feeling a man's strength on the other end.

Pace, his brains still scrambled by the sudden racket that had wakened him, drew his Colt and thumbed two fast shots through the trapdoor.

He was rewarded by a yelp of surprise and the sound of running feet.

"Hell, it's the deacon," Lake said. He was looking over the top of the rail. "Damn, he's seen me."

That last was made obvious when a bullet *ting*ed off the side of the bell and a second chipped timber close to Lake's head.

Pace stepped to the rail. Immediately a bullet

split the air an inch from his left ear. He caught only a fleeting glimpse of the deacon before Lake reached up and pulled him down.

"Don't gunfight him, boy," Lake said. "He'll kill you fer sure."

"My God," Jess said, her nose wrinkling, "what's that awful smell?"

"It's the smell of cholera," Pace said. "The deacon is leaving a trail of it behind him."

Jess said nothing, but she looked stunned, as though the full horror of the disease had just struck her.

"Where are the Peacock boys?" Lake said.

"I didn't see them," Pace said. "They drank the well water and if they're not sick yet, they will be real soon."

"Then all we have to do is wait," Jess said.

Pace nodded. "Seems like. Unless they hurry and come up with something that surprises the hell out of us."

His face fell. "Damn it, the ladder."

He waved Jess and Lake away from the trap-door, then opened it a few inches.

"Like I thought, it's gone," he said. "Damn the deacon for a son of a bitch. He moved it."

"How do we get down from here, Sammy?" Jess said.

"We'll use the rope."

"I've never done that before," Jess said. "I mean, climb down a bell rope."

"Me neither," Pace said. "But it's got to beat the hell out of jumping."

"What do you see, Sam?" Lake said.

"The street's empty."

Pace waited a few moments, then said, "Mash, take a look at this."

Lake peered over the top of the rail. "What am I supposed to see?"

"To the west, in the hills. There it goes again."

"Yeah, I saw the flash."

"Reckon it's the army?"

"Could be, but Apaches also use mirror signals."

"There's plenty of dust kicking up," Pace said.

Lake nodded. "Twenty, maybe thirty riders."

"They're not moving in our direction."

"Army or Apache, seems like they found something more interesting than us to occupy their time."

Jess kneeled beside Pace. "We could signal them, fire some shots."

"We could," Pace said, "if it's the army. But suppose it's Apaches? We'd be in even more danger than we are now."

Jess had no answer for that and again lapsed into silence.

The long summer day burned on. The sun seared its way across the sky, and to the west buzzards lazily rode the air currents.

The bell tower smelled of pine resin, hot iron, and human sweat.

Pace sat and fetched his back against the rail.

"It's all quiet at the saloon," he said. "We'll wait until just before dark and make our move."

"What's your plan?" Lake said.

"Apart from getting down from here, I don't have one."

Neither Lake nor Jess commented on that, and Pace smiled.

"If all's quiet until dark, then I'll reckon the cholera has done our work for us."

"Is it really so quick?" Jess said, shivering despite the heat of the day. "Alive in the morning. Dead come suppertime."

"It depends on the strain, or so Doc Anderson told me before he was finally took. When the cholera was killing a dozen people a day in Requiem, the doc said he'd seen the disease in Baltimore, Memphis, Washington, and a couple of other cities, but he reckoned the cholera in the well down there was the most"—Pace racked his memory for the right word—"the most *virulent* he'd ever come across."

"What's that word mean, Sam?" Lake said.

" 'Virulent'? I guess it means real bad for a person."

"Then why didn't he just say 'real bad for a person'?"

"Because he was a doctor, and doctors use

words nobody's ever heard before. That's why they become doctors, so they can use words like 'virulent.' "

"Do you think they're all already dead down there, Sammy?" Jess said.

"Yes. I believe they are, or close to it."

But then the sound of gunshots gave the lie to Pace's confident statement.

Chapter 45

Deacon Santee staggered into the saloon, bringing with him a stench that quickly filled the entire room with a noxious vapor.

"They shot at me," he said. "That damned white trash shot at a sick man."

He looked around, his eyes becoming accustomed to the gloom.

One of the Peacocks sat on a chair against the far wall. He moaned as pain stabbed at him again and again, vileness pooling around his feet, fed by the stinking liquids that still ran uncontrollably from his body.

Two of the other brothers stood on either side of a table, a man lying on his back between them.

The deacon took a couple of steps forward, but then stopped.

"Is that the dummy?" he said.

"He was the last born of us and frail," a brother said. "He would not eat, fasting constantly, as though famine stalked the land."

Clutched by pain, the deacon swayed against the bar, holding on to stay upright. He felt something vile run down his legs.

He bit back a surge of pain, then said, "A man's got to eat or he dies."

"Famine didn't kill him," the brother said. "It was you who killed him."

"It was the brandy," Santee said. "I reckon it had gone bad."

"Idiot," the brother said, "it was the water. The well is poisoned, yet you told us the water was good to drink."

"Hell, I drank it my own self," the deacon said. "How was I to know it was pizened?"

"You should have known," the brother said. "We'll all be dead soon, and this town will be our funeral pyre." He waved a hand. "Up there, in the bell tower, we will find dogs to lie at our feet."

The deacon was burning with fever, battered by pain, and his bowels were melting, running down his legs as a foul-smelling effluent.

He doubted that he could remain on his feet much longer, and he was in no shape for a gunfight.

"Well, see, about that dying business," he said, his mouth bone dry. "The pizen hasn't been made that can kill Deacon Santee."

"Yet, rest assured, you will die with the rest of us," the brother said. "Die now, die later. The choice is yours."

The deacon didn't like that last one bit. It was a pretty obvious threat. This was shaping up to become a draw-and-shoot, and, sick and trembling as he was, he wasn't sure if he'd be the last one standing when the smoke cleared.

Then, suddenly, his mind was made up for him.

The other Peacock, who'd been standing at the table and so far had remained silent, groaned. He lurched backward, clutched at his belly, and slumped over, body fluids noisily erupting from him.

The deacon took his chance.

He drew and fired at the brother who'd accused him of knowing the well was poisoned.

"Take that and be damned to ye," he roared, his voice exploding with pent-up anger and fear.

The Peacock brother took the bullet, a solid torso hit, and staggered, scarlet blood frothing on the front of his white shirt.

The deacon headed for the batwings, firing on the move.

Another hit.

His target went down on his knees, but the man's gun came up, fast, but unsteady, the muzzle wavering.

Something slammed into the deacon's left shoulder, shocking in its brute force and intensity.

Hit hard, he paused by the doors and his gaze scanned the room.

Santee was not one to take a bullet and let the man who shot him walk the earth.

His fevered eyes went to the kneeling man on the floor, dismissed him, and moved to the back of the saloon. The brother who'd been sitting on a chair against the wall was on his feet, his gun straight out in front of him.

The deacon fired, fired again.

His bullets chipped timber as the Peacock dived to his right side and crashed to the floor, scrabbling out of sight behind a table.

Santee was angry, but he let the man go. His time would come later.

He backed to the door and eyed the kneeling Peacock. The man was staring at nothing, blood trickling down his chin. His gun was still in his hand, but seemed too heavy for him to lift.

"Son of a bitch," the deacon said.

He drew from his left holster and emptied the gun into the dying Peacock. Coldly, Santee watched the man roll over and lie still on his side.

"Damn all of you!" he yelled into the smoke-streaked saloon. "Damn all of you to hell."

The deacon staggered into the street and made for his horse at the barbershop hitch rail.

The left side of his chest was soaked in blood, he stank, and he was on fire with fever. He

195

reckoned everything that was inside him had turned to liquid and would be gone by now. But it was not. It kept coming, running down his legs, leaving a track behind him like the slime trail of an obscene snail.

Twice he stumbled, and had to claw to his feet again.

The hot sun pounded him, baking his unspeakable stench to his body, and he had a raging thirst.

His horse was close. Not far, only a few steps.

Very soon, he'd be with his women. They'd attend to him, make him better. Wash him, give him clean clothes, set him in the shade, and quench his thirst with cool water. Be loving wives.

He smiled.

The deacon would be himself again.

Chapter 46

"What do you think, Sam?"

Pace met Lake's eyes. "Five men went into the saloon, there was a gunfight, and only one of them left. The deacon. What does that tell us?"

"Seems like the deacon done fer them Peacock boys, them as were still alive."

Pace nodded. "Yep, seems like."

"He was movin' slow, the deacon. I think he'd taken a hit."

"Could be. But he's dying of the cholera anyhow."

"I don't think I seen that much shit since—"

"Mash! Please, stop it," Jess said.

"Sorry," Lake said.

"It's disgusting."

"Cholera is disgusting," Pace said. "Everybody who gets it dies hard. Nobody passes away with dignity."

"Then if I get it, shoot me," Jess said. "Put me out of my misery."

"The cholera's down there, Miz Jess," Lake said. "It ain't up here."

"Down there, up here, I don't give a damn. I want out of this hell town," the woman said. "I'm willing to take my chances with the Apaches."

"Me too, I guess," Lake said. He looked at Pace. "How about you, Sam?"

"I'll make that decision later," Pace said, his eyes guarded.

"There's no decision to make, Sammy," Jess said. "You're getting out of here with us."

"Jess is right, boy," Lake said. "If you stay here it's all up with you. You'll always be crazy as a loon."

"We'll see," Pace said. "Until I come down to it, a man never knows which way the pickle will squirt."

Lake and Jess locked eyes, each aware of what the other was thinking.

Sam Pace continued to walk a fine line between sanity and madness. It would take very little to tip him over the edge into that hellish place where he'd spent the past three years.

"Well, this is interesting," Pace said.

Lake joined him and they both peered over the top of the railing.

"What the hell is he doin'?" the old man said.

"Looking this way."

"Hell, boy, I can see that."

One of the Peacock brothers stood outside the saloon door, his back against the wall for support. The man looked ill, close to death ill, and it was obvious that he could barely stand.

"Surrendering?" Lake suggested. "Reckon he's had enough and wants to give up, Sam?"

That question was answered when the Peacock drew his revolver and thumbed off two fast shots. His bullets stung the bell, then whined away like angry hornets.

Pace drew his Colt and fired back. He missed, but the Peacock brother staggered back into the saloon and faded into shadow.

"What the hell was that fer?" Lake said.

"He wanted to make sure we were still here," Pace said. "That's what it was fer."

"I think he's sceered, Sam," Lake said. "I

say we go down there and have it out with him."

"There may be others."

"Yeah, but you can bet the farm they'll be as sick as he is."

Pace was silent for a few moments, then said, "I don't know. He looked spry enough after I shot at him."

"He also hit the bell, twice," Jess said. "I'd say that's good shooting for a dying man."

"For any man," Pace allowed.

The day faded and the light changed from searing white to pale lilac. Shadows appeared in the street, and angles of thin darkness appeared in the alleys between the buildings.

Mash Lake had been sitting in silence, but now his face wrinkled in thought.

"Hey, Sam," he said, "if we clumb down the rope we could come up on them by surprise, like," he said. "Gun them damn Peacock boys before they even know what's hit them."

"Climb down the rope and we'll take nobody by surprise," Pace said. "The bell will ring so loud, folks will hear it in the next county."

He reached out and thumbed off a piece of wood from the railing, then crumbled it in his hand. He let the pieces fall to the floor.

"Rotten," Pace said. "Even if we untied the rope from the bell beam, none of the timber up here is strong enough to hold it."

"I never thought o' that," Lake said. He shook his head. "I guess every jackass thinks he's got hoss sense until he's told otherwise."

Jess brushed a strand of hair from her eyes. Her forehead was sheened with sweat and her dress showed damp at the armpits and clung tight to her breasts.

"All right, Sammy, you didn't like Mash's suggestion," she said. "Let's hear yours."

"We wait until full dark, then make our break," Pace said. "I'll go first and then replace the ladder. If any of the Peacocks are still alive by then, I'll hold them off until you and Mash climb down."

"And then?" Jess said.

"And then we hightail it out of Requiem. Sometimes it's a sight safer to pull your freight than your gun."

"Suppose the Peacocks come after us?" Lake said.

"If they're not dead, they'll be almighty sick. Them boys won't come after us."

Pace looked over the rail and studied the saloon. There was no sign of life and no sound, only the *tick-tick-tick* of the batwing doors blowing back and forth against each other in a rising east wind.

"In another hour or two, we'll have nothing to fear from the Peacocks," he said. "They were dead men the moment they put the dipper to their lips and drank from the well."

Chapter 47

By the time the sun began its drop to the horizon and the sky streaked red, two of the Peacock brothers were dead, and the others barely holding on to life.

After cholera strikes, it doesn't let go. It torments its victims all the way to the grave, and the dying is not quick and never easy.

The dead brothers lay in pools of their own filth that reeked of rotten fish, the distinctive aroma of the bacterium *Vibrio cholerae*. Swollen tongues stuck out of their stick-dry mouths and even in death fever burned in their eyes, as though the disease was reluctant to give up even the ravaged carcasses of its victims.

The surviving Peacocks sat at a table, naked, stripped of the filthy clothing that had clung, stuck, and cleaved to their stinking bodies.

Their beautiful Colts, tuned like fine violins by a German gunsmith, they'd cast aside on the floor, the need for them gone.

Fire.

Now their weapon was fire.

"Soon," one of the brothers said. "It must be soon."

"Come the darkness," the other said.

"We'll be too weak by then, maybe dead."

"No, we'll find the strength. Sometimes the dead can walk."

The man waved a hand in the direction of the church. "Over there is one who has done us much harm. We'll watch him burn and then we'll hound his soul through the canyons of hell for all eternity."

"And we'll be five again."

"Yes. Five. As we were before the man called Lake came into our lives."

The brother who'd spoken first rose to his feet and immediately collapsed on the floor. He convulsed as a wave of pain hit him, then lay still for a few moments.

His brother didn't ask him how he was because there was no point. He already knew. Like himself, his brother was dying one faltering heartbeat at a time.

Finally the man on the floor began to crawl. After an agonizing length of time, he reached the cans of coal oil that the deacon had left against the wall.

He grabbed a can by its handle and dragged it with him to the saloon door. There he stopped and his skull face split in a grotesque grin. He turned and looked at his brother.

"I can do it. When the time comes, I'll be able."

The sitting brother's eyes moved to the door. It was still not dark, but the orange sun hung low in the sky and the shadows were lengthening.

"Not long, brother," he said. "It will soon be dark."

"I long to see them burn," the Peacock at the door said. "We've seen it before many times, have we not? How the skin bubbles, the hair blazes, the eyes scorch out of the head as though rammed by red-hot pokers."

"And they scream, brother. They shriek and wail and gambol about in a dance and it always makes me laugh."

The man clutched on to the table, clenched his teeth against pain and the sudden, abominable flux that gushed, spluttering, from his body. It was a full five minutes before he could find the strength to talk again.

Finally he said, "Not long now before all the fires of hell descend on this accursed place."

Above the saloon, a red-tailed hawk quartered the sky and its shrill hunting cry slashed through the evening quiet like a razor.

Chapter 48

Deacon Santee heard the screech of a hawk above the tree canopy, but did not lift his head to look. Nor could he.

He was sick, sicker than he'd ever been in his life.

Right now he should be in bed, tended by his women, not lying across the neck of a horse, trusting that the animal was less lost than he was.

He was traveling toward the setting sun, in the right direction.

Once out of these infernal trees, he'd know where he was headed.

Camp couldn't be too far away now.

He sniffed, sniffed again.

Wood smoke. Praise the Lord, it was wood smoke!

Not far, then. A mile. Maybe less.

The horse stopped dead in its tracks, so suddenly that the deacon had to grab on to its neck to avoid a tumble.

He tried to kick the animal into a walk, but it stood stock-still, refusing to budge.

Then he smelled it, a stench different to his own rotten-fish stink. Sweeter. And close.

It took a tremendous effort of will, but Santee managed to raise himself into a sitting position in the saddle.

Then he saw what his horse had seen.

His sons Gideon and Zedock.

Or what was left of them.

There was not a shred of human decency in Deacon Santee, nor any depth of paternal feeling. His sons had been sired on whores and he'd always believed he had the ability to hammer out more should the need arise.

But something stirred in him as he watched his boys twist in the wind, their hands rawhide-tied to a tree limb.

Love, pity, empathy, all were alien emotions to the deacon, yet, in small measure certainly, he felt them now, fragile and faint, like a butterfly fluttering its wings in his belly.

He kneed his horse closer to the tree. Nearby, a wisp of smoke rose from an ashy fire. The burning sticks that had been rammed into his sons' eyes had been lit there.

Their bellies had been cut open and curling blue entrails tangled down their legs and spilled onto the ground.

Was it then, or before, that they screamed? Their mouths were still open now, but the screams were silent.

Gideon and Zedock had been given a death worse than cholera. Worse than anything.

His breath wheezing in his chest, Santee pulled his knife, leaned out of the saddle, and cut his sons down. The bodies thudded to the grass, one on top of the other, sprawled and untidy, and lay still.

The smoldering fire told the deacon that the Apaches were close.

He knew that their sense of smell was keener than a white man's and that they followed the scent the way a wild animal does.

The stench of rotting fish that clung to his body would leave an easy trail.

He had to get back to the wagons. Surely some of the hands had made it through with the herd.

Once again, Santee gave his horse its head, vaguely aware that it followed an old game trail through the wild oaks.

The grass and trees were greener than he ever remembered them. Above the leaf canopy the sky had shaded into a lemon color, and the final flare of the dying sun tinted the few clouds burnished gold.

After . . . the deacon didn't know how long . . . the trees gave way to brush, and then to grass.

Ahead of him spread the valley with its S-shaped creek. Harcourt's tent still stood and he saw a few grazing cattle.

It was a peaceful scene, and the deacon raised his voice in a joyful shout of hallelujah. The good Lord had shown him the way.

He was home.

The Apaches knew the smell of cholera and stayed well away from the white man who tainted the earth with his fish stink.

But they watched him, their black eyes glittering, as they let him pass through their ranks to the valley.

Chapter 49

Deacon Santee found two dead men in the grass, separated by about twenty paces. Both had been shot multiple times, most of their wounds in the back.

He drew rein and looked around him.

It took a while because his sight was blurred, but he spotted the bodies of three more punchers, like the others widely spread apart.

Several cows grazed by the river, one of them a longhorn, but the rest of the herd was scattered to hell and gone, as though they'd dropped off the edge of the world.

The signs were written in burning letters four feet tall and the deacon had no trouble reading them.

There had been a running fight with Apaches, and his sons had been killed early. The rest of the punchers had tried to make it back to camp and had died after they crossed the creek.

As for the herd, it had spooked and most of the cattle would still be running.

His eyes had once been far-seeing, but now, as the cholera ravaged him, the deacon couldn't make out his wagons.

But they'd be there, he knew. He had no

illusions about what he'd find, but then, hope is often the last thing to die in a man.

Santee kneed his horse forward, riding through the long summer twilight and the silence that lay softly on the land.

The breeze felt cool on his face and tasted of pine and he heard coyotes yip in some faint, faraway place.

The deacon rode on, fearful of what he'd find, fearful of the death that awaited him. Fearful of what might come thereafter.

It was worse than he'd imagined, worse than anyone could have imagined.

A man can use a woman hard, but in the end, if he's considerate, little harm is done.

But Apache warriors had ways of using a woman where much harm was done and consideration for the woman's well-being didn't enter into their way of thinking.

And so it was with the deacon's wives.

The women lay on their backs, legs spread wide, their naked bodies bone white in the half-light except where dried blood crusted black.

Among them lay the body of the vaquero who'd helped Santee shoot Beau Harcourt into collops. The scrap iron head of a war lance was buried deep in the man's chest and he'd been scalped.

But he'd sold his life dearly, the ground around his body littered with empty shells from his Winchester.

The deacon half stepped, half fell from the saddle.

He moved from body to body, forcing himself to experience the horror in full measure to feed his growing anger.

He felt no grief. No sense of loss.

He took women only for the physical pleasure they provided. Emotional bonds did not interest the deacon in the least.

But ownership did.

The gals had been his'n. And the Apaches had taken them away from him.

Now he would exact the women's blood price in lead.

That day Deacon James J. Santee sought redemption of a sort, trusting that belted men would talk of him in later days as a man who had sand enough to exact a reckoning.

He drew his guns and looked to where the Apaches had gathered, sensing that true nobility lies in being superior to your previous self.

As he sought revenge for his dead wives and braced himself for his last fight, the deacon was about to do something finer than he'd ever done before in his hunted, violent existence.

And in the end he perhaps found, at least in small measure, his lost nobility.

Chapter 50

The deacon staggered across the short grass, a gun in each hand, muzzles pointing to the painted sky.

As though anger had cleared his vision, he saw the Apaches now, gathered on the bank of the creek.

He glanced at the sky. It would be dark soon. A single star shone in the east, heralding the coming night. It was a pleasant evening and he felt like a man taking a stroll along a city boulevard.

He walked on, leaving a loathsome trail behind him as his rupturing guts emptied again and again.

Every step weakened him, and he did not know how many were left to him.

Enough.

Soon he'd be among the savages, where he would play hob.

His voice, weak, thin, reedy, rose in song.

Mine eyes have seen the glory of the coming of the Lord,
He is trampling out the vintage where the grapes of wrath are stored . . .

Now he was marching, by God. Marching to glory.

He fired his guns. Two fast shots that racketed across the hush of the evening.

"I'm a-comin' for y'all!" he yelled. "Hear me! The deacon's on his way."

Steadily now, he triggered his revolvers, a rolling thunder of gunfire from the weapons of a master.

Mine eyes have seen the glory . . .

A bullet crashed into the deacon's left thigh and shattered bone. He dropped to a knee, staggered to his feet, and walked on, gritting his teeth.

He sang his war song like that, the words wrenching out of him.

Of the coming of the Lord . . .

Two bullets now, fired with fine accuracy from .44-40 Winchesters.

One ball slammed into the deacon's chest, the other lower, deep in his belly.

He fell to his knees, triggered his guns.

Empty clicks.

Bullets hammered into him. Shredded him. Destroyed him.

The deacon took a last look at the sky, caught a glimpse of something terrifying, then screamed and fell on his face.

His body erupted one last time, but Deacon Santee was already dead.

The Apaches left him where he lay and did not go near his body.

They knew and feared the ways of cholera.

Chapter 51

"Damn it, Mash, hold it for a while longer," Sam Pace said. "It'll be dark soon."

"Man can't hold what's not in his hand," Lake said.

"Hell, Mash, piss over the side," Jess said. "I don't mind."

"I do," Pace said. "The Peacocks will shoot his damn fool pecker off."

"When a man's got to go, a man's got to go," Lake said.

He stood, turned his back to Jess, and fumbled with his fly. He leaned against the rail and sent a steaming stream of piss hissing over the side.

Lake talked over his shoulder.

"Had to stop an' piss in the middle of a gunfight oncet, up in the Nevada Slate Ridge country," he said. He nodded. "Yep, I recollect that like it was yesstidy."

"We don't want to hear about it, Mash," Pace said, irritated.

"I do," Jess said. "How did you manage it, Mash, without getting shot?"

"Well," Lake said, "me an' this gold miner, English feller by the name of Giles St. John, got into it over a silver watch he claimed I stole from him. He called me out and we stood in the street and took pots at each other. But, after a spell, I held up my hand and said, 'Giles, hold your fire. I got to take a piss, get rid of some of the beer in my gut.' Giles, he says, 'You go right ahead, Mash. I'm a British gentleman and I won't shoot until you've finished.' "

Lake sighed, buttoned up, and said, "Hell, I needed that."

"What about Giles St. John?" Jess said.

"What about him?" Lake said.

"What happened after you stopped to take a piss and he told you he wouldn't shoot, him being a gentleman and all?"

"Oh yeah. Well, I'm standing there, letting it go, and the damned limey took another pot at me. Damn near blew my head off. So I buttoned up and said, "Giles, you're a no-good son of a bitch, an' low down.' "

Lake sat, and settled his back against the rail. "I drawed my revolver again, and cut loose. Come mighty close. Then ol' Giles, he figures he's had enough for one day and takes off running, and I ain't seen him from that day to this."

Lake shrugged. "Of course, we was both drunk

at the time, so I never did hold that pot against him none."

"So the moral of the story is: Don't drink a belly-load of beer before a gunfight," Jess said.

Lake smiled and nodded. "Young lady, them's words of wisdom. Beer an' gunfighting just don't mix."

"Mash," Pace said, "please, if you ever get the urge again, don't tell us any more big windies."

"It ain't a windy, Sam. It happened just like I tole you."

"I think Mash's story is easier to believe than three people sitting in a bell tower waiting for dark," Jess said.

"Me too," Mash said. He eyed Pace. "Huh! Big windy, my ass."

Night erased the last traces of daylight from Requiem.

A ghost town casts still shadows. But it makes the surrounding darkness restless, on edge, as though it's waiting for something to happen, perhaps the misty midnight appearance of the people who once lived there.

The wind was from the east, coming off old, stone mountains, bringing with it the scent of pine and the ability to make placid men angry.

Sam Pace stood at the rail of the bell tower, his eyes searching into the night. Nothing moved and there was no sound.

Lake stepped to his side. "See anything?"

Pace shook his head.

"Then, just like you said, the cholera's done for them Peacocks," Lake said.

"Seems like."

"Does that mean we can get down from here?" Jess said.

"It do," Lake answered. He looked at Pace. "Don't it?"

Pace made no answer, his head turned, eyes fixed on the saloon.

"Hell, boy, what do you see?" Lake said.

"I don't know what I see."

"Describe it, Sammy," Jess said. She sounded tense.

"White," Pace said. "I thought I saw something white move near the saloon door."

"A coyote?" Jess said.

"Maybe."

Pace was silent for a while, then said, "You know what I think it was?"

Jess and Lake stared at him.

"I think maybe it was a naked man on all fours, crawling along the boardwalk in the shadow of the saloon wall."

"What the hell does that mean?" Jess said.

"It means two things. One, all the Peacocks aren't dead."

"And the other?" Jess said.

"The other is that we could be in a heap of trouble."

Chapter 52

Sam Pace lifted his rifle to his shoulder.

He aimed just to the right of the saloon door where the wall met the boardwalk.

Levering the Winchester from his shoulder, he dusted shots along the angled shadow from the door to the end of the boardwalk. His bullets splintered timber from the walk and thudded into the saloon wall.

The racket of the rifle roused Requiem from slumber.

The Peacock brothers' high-strung horses yanked away from the saloon hitch rail. The startled animals uprooted the supporting posts and galloped down the street, dragging the rail with them.

Echoes slammed through the alleys and town buildings, booming like muffled drums.

Lake's eyes probed the darkness, his ears ringing.

"Did you get him, Sam?" he said, too loudly.

"Hell, I don't know," Pace said. "It's too dark to see. Where's the damned moon?"

He listened into the night, heard nothing.

"Like Jess says, maybe it was just a coyote," Lake said.

Pace said nothing, and the woman said, "Sammy, you're scaring the hell out of me. Let's get down from here."

"I don't want to dangle from a rope with the Peacocks taking shots at me," Pace said. "We'll wait for a spell."

"Damn it, Sammy, wait for what?" Jess said.

"I don't know."

The woman was silent for a moment, as though she'd just been slapped.

"Right, that's it," she said. "I'm climbing down the rope."

"Wait!" Pace said.

He smelled it now. The sulfurous stink of rotten eggs.

"Mash, was that you?" Jess said, her nose wrinkling.

"Hell no. I—"

"It's coal oil," Pace yelled. "Damn it, they're going to burn the church out from under us."

Pace smelled smoke, then saw the first flames lick the side of the church. The fire reached higher. And higher.

The timber that framed the building, especially the heavier beams that supported the roof, had baked beneath four summers of relentless sun and they were tinder dry. The fire quickly took hold and the church torched, blazed, roared as though in mortal pain.

Black smoke shrouded the belfry, and the air became hard to breathe.

"Damn it," Lake said, "I'm gonna jump."

"No!" Pace yelled. "You damned fool, you'll break your legs."

He dragged Lake toward the bell rope. "Climb down."

"How the hell do I manage that?" Lake said.

Behind him, flames were shooting through the floorboards.

Pace shoved the rope into Lake's hands. "Here. Learn as you go."

The old man aired out his lungs, cursing Pace and the mother who bore him, but he took the rope. He clambered down, using only his hands, and his head bobbed out of sight.

"Now you, Jess," Pace said.

The woman needed no second bidding. The entire church was ablaze, and the supporting timbers of the bell tower cracked and creaked, threatening to collapse into the inferno.

Pace watched Jess slide down the rope and took one last glance around him.

What he saw chilled him to the bone.

Sparks from the burning church had jumped to the roof of the saloon and the rod and gun store next to it. Both buildings, parched tinderboxes, smoked, and here and there flames fluttered like scarlet moths.

"No!" Pace yelled.

His town was burning to death.

Chapter 53

Sam Pace grabbed the rope and started his downward climb.

He was still ten feet above the ground when the bell tower collapsed.

Flaming timbers plummeted around Pace and a beam slammed into the top of his left shoulder, numbing his arm. He let go of the rope and fell heavily to the smoldering ground.

The weight of the heavy iron bell forced the shattered wreckage of the tower to tumble into the street—and saved Pace from further injury from falling beams or the bell itself.

But fire rippled across the ceiling of the church and hemmed him in on all sides as the walls blazed. Trapped by sheets of flame, Pace felt tongues of fire lashing at him, the heat threatening to scorch out his lungs.

Fire is a good servant but a bad master, and Pace felt a surge of panic as flames lashed at him. Blinded by smoke, he turned to his right and, limping on a left ankle that had taken the brunt of his fall, ran for his life.

Pace lowered his head and hit a shifting scarlet and gold wall. He splintered through burning timbers and what was left of the charred framing and hit the grass rolling.

He felt fire rip at his back, staggered to his feet, and tore off his burning shirt. Then he ran again, away from the church. Behind him the entire building collapsed with a roar, flames shooting high into the night sky.

Pace limped into the street, and the sight that greeted him caught the breath in his throat.

The whole town was on fire, from the saloon all the way to the barbershop. The east wind had picked up and spawned a roaring firestorm that cartwheeled through the buildings.

Worse was to come.

As Pace watched, the fire finally found the stacked barrels of gunpowder in the rod and gun shop. With a tremendous roar, the roof of the store was lifted clean off. The blast leveled the walls and scorched and splintered timbers hurtled across the street.

Pace felt the explosion like a gigantic fist, its punch powerful enough to knock him on his back.

For a couple of minutes he lay where he was, stunned. Then slowly, painfully, he rose to his feet.

The sky above Requiem had shaded from midnight blue to cherry red, barred by a dozen columns of sooty black. The wind fanned flames that devoured Requiem like wolves, picking the town clean to the bone.

Sam Pace groaned and fell to his knees, a sorrowing penitent at a sacrificial altar.

His town was gone. And with it, the reason for his existence.

Pace saw the movement out of the corner of his vision, the slow crawl of a white worm. He lifted his head and his eyes narrowed, focused, clutched at a fistful of night.

The worm crept, slithered, slid away from the burning church, its way lit by fire.

Sam Pace rose to his feet. He drew his Colt and limped toward the worm, tall and terrible, his naked chest splashed by scarlet shadow, the hollows of his eyes deep in darkness.

The worm, pale, covered in filth from its own body, stopped and looked at him. It raised a hand, in a plea for mercy or in defiance, Pace would never know.

"Which of them Peacocks are you?" Pace said, looking down at the man.

The mouth in the skull face opened, smiled. "Pestilence."

Pace nodded. "Then go back to hell, damn you."

He emptied his gun into the man, and was still thumbing the clicking hammer when Jess grabbed his arm and gently pulled him away.

Chapter 54

Come daylight, the wind still came from the east. It nosed around the cremated remains of Requiem, now a charred skeleton of ruined buildings that framed crazily leaning spars rising out of a gray sea of ash.

Wisps of smoke still drifted from the wreckage, the sad remnants of the town's funeral pyre.

Sam Pace and Jess stood in the street and gazed at the carnage the fire had wrought.

Pace was silent, his face like stone, and Jess's heart went out to him.

"I'm sorry, Sammy," she said, looking at him, "so sorry that your town is gone." Then, hopefully: "There's no reason left for you to stay."

Pace said nothing, but after a few long moments he said, "Are all the Peacock brothers dead?"

Jess nodded. "Mash says he saw one burn in the church. I guess the two others died in the saloon."

"Where is Mash?"

"He left to go look for the Peacock horses. He told you that."

"I didn't hear him."

Jess put her hand on Pace's arm. "Are you all right, Sammy?"

"I'm fine, just fine."

The woman's face was blackened by smoke, her eyes red-rimmed, still smarting.

"When Mash finds the horses, we can get out of here," she said. "Mash said Snowflake is a big Mormon settlement and we'll be safe from the Apaches there."

Jess put her hand on Pace's forearm. "I think we could make it, you and me. I mean, be happy together."

Pace said nothing. He looked around him, his eyes distant.

Then, like a man waking from a dream, he turned and smiled, a vague smile, remote as the far mountains.

"I must stay here because the people will rebuild," he said. "That is the way of western men and women. They endure. After hard times they straighten their backs, pick up and start all over again. It's been that way in the past and it will be that way in the future."

Jess moved a step toward Pace, hesitated a heartbeat, then threw her arms around his neck.

"Sammy, hang on," she said. "You'll be fine when we get to Snowflake. You'll feel better. I know you will."

Pace gently disengaged the woman and looked around him.

"I thought I'd lost everything," he said. "But I haven't. This is still a town, my town, and it will be reborn out of the ashes."

Jess said nothing. Suddenly she felt an emotion that was a close kin to despair and it cut through her like a blade.

Mash Lake shook his head. "Nary a sign of them, Sam. Apaches would've jumped at the chance to nab them big American studs."

"Mash, what do we do now?" Jess asked, alarm in her voice.

Lake smiled. "We walk, little lady."

"Without horses you'll never make it," Pace said. "How many Apaches do you think there are between here and Snowflake?"

"Well, hell, boy, we can't stay where we're at," Lake said.

The two men had accompanied Jess to the creek. They sat on the bank while she kneeled by the water, splashing her face, neck, and breasts.

"You can stay right here, Mash," Pace said. "When the folks come back, you and Jess can find work helping them rebuild." He smiled. "I might even make you my deputy if you steer clear of the whiskey."

Now it was Lake's turn to show alarm.

"Are you goin' crazy on me again, boy?" he said.

"Mash," Jess said, "leave him alone."

"But he's cuttin' loco close again, Jess," Lake said.

The woman dried her hands on her dress, then did up the buttons over her breasts.

"Sammy is coming with us to Snowflake," she said. "He'll be fine once he's away from this awful place." She hesitated just a moment, then said, "I'll take care of him."

Pace shook his head. "No, I told you, I'm staying right here. Requiem is my town and now it needs me more than ever."

"Son," Lake said, his voice gentle, "there is no town."

Pace smiled. "Well, that's where you're wrong, old man."

He rose to his feet and looked toward the piled ruins.

"I can see it," he said, his gaze glowing. "I can see the new buildings, all the tall stores and saloons and maybe a new church. The signs will be fresh painted and hang on chains outside every door and people will go in and out, the womenfolk with packages in their hands, the men stopping in the street to talk crop yields and cattle prices."

Pace grinned and pointed. "Jess, Mash, look. Can't you see it? The town of Requiem, new-aborned from the ashes. It's there. All you have to do is look."

Mash got to his feet and stood beside him.

"Sam, if they're to last, buildings need a firm foundation," he said. "And so does a man. If he don't have that, he'll sink into the ground and be lost forever."

He turned and waved in Jess's direction. "Over there is a woman who can give you that foundation, boy. Go with her so you don't sink any deeper into craziness."

Pace shook his head. "You just don't see it, do you, Mash?"

The wrinkled planes of Lake's face stiffened. "I see what I see, boy. An' I don't like any of it."

Chapter 55

Mash Lake carried a burlap sack over his shoulder, bulging with the blackened cans of food he'd scavenged from the burned-out husk of the general store. He carried his rifle in his left hand.

Beside him, Jess had a couple of blankets tied to her back and she wore a battered hat Pace had given her.

"Change your minds," he said. "You won't make it."

Lake shook his head. "Sam, I've fit Apaches afore and I reckon I've got their measure. We can't stay here, boy. We'd starve to death if'n the cholera didn't get us first."

Pace looked at the woman. "Jess?"

"I'm going with Mash, Sammy. This is a terrible, cursed place. I can't stay here a minute longer."

Her face was strained, the plea in her voice almost a sob.

"Sammy, come with us. I'll be a good woman to you, I promise."

Pace smiled. "I reckon not. This is where I belong."

Jess had realized hours before that further argument was useless. Now she accepted what was happening and gave up the struggle.

"Then take care of yourself, Sammy," she said.

Pace nodded. "You too, Jess."

Lake stuck out a hand. "Good luck, boy. Don't go too crazy, you hear?"

"I'll try not to," Pace said. He held Lake's hand a moment longer than a handshake demanded.

He watched them go, kept his eyes on them until they dissolved into shimmering distance and passing time.

Pace knew they wouldn't make it to Snowflake alive.

He was sure Mash Lake, an old Indian fighter, knew as well.

Maybe Jess had a different idea, but he'd never

been any good at reading women and couldn't guess what was in her mind.

She'd lived a hard, degraded life and Pace felt she deserved better than that. But worst of all, her death would go unnoticed and unmourned, and that was the greatest tragedy of all.

He looked into the distance, empty now, and lifted a hand in farewell.

"Good luck, my friends," he said.

Pace walked along the street, past blackened heaps of charred timber, all that was left of his town. Only the livery stable still stood. The fire had been content to scorch its roof and walls and do no other damage.

He looked inside and noticed a can of red paint, and that gave him an idea.

Pace kicked out a pine board from the stable wall, then found a paintbrush. He laid the plank flat on the ground, kneeled, and wrote DANGER CHOLERA WELL.

He stood and admired his handiwork. It would do just fine.

Pace walked back to the well and laid the board across the parapet.

He nodded, satisfied. Now nobody else would drink the damned water.

The sun began its climb into the morning sky as Pace walked down the street, past the livery and in the direction of the cemetery.

Now all he could do was wait, and there was no better place than a shady spot near his wife and child.

When he reached the site of the mass grave, he unbuckled his gun and let it drop to the ground. Then he sat, his chin on his knees, and began his vigil.

The sun left and the moon found him there.

Then the sun again.

But Sam Pace did not move.

He was waiting . . . for the return of the living . . . or the dead.

Historical Note

Cholera was an ever-present danger in Western cow towns, where outhouses and cattle pens were often situated too close to the water supply.

The great Asiatic cholera outbreak of June and July 1867 killed three hundred people in booming Ellsworth, Kansas, and helped hasten the town's demise as a major cattle center.

Wagon trains were particularly susceptible to the disease. In bad years, two-thirds of the emigrants on the Oregon Trail succumbed to cholera, a greater mortality rate than from any other cause.

There was no cure and people could go from healthy to dead in a matter of hours.

Sometimes the pioneers received a proper burial, but many were simply abandoned in their beds by the side of the trail, to die alone.

Emigrant John Clark later described such a scene: "One woman and two men lay dead on the grass and some more ready to die. Women and children crying, some hunting medicine and none to be found. With heartfelt sorrow, we looked around for some time until I felt unwell myself. Got up and moved forward one mile, so to be out of hearing of crying and suffering."

To prevent the disease, emigrants were advised to "carry a small bottle of tincture of camphor and a few lumps of sugar in your pocket . . . and when you have any pain or disorder in your bowels, take three or four drops (of the camphor) on sugar."

Of course, by the time you had "pain or disorder in your bowels," you were already dead.

The Mormon settlement of Snowflake, Arizona, was established in 1878 by William J. Flake and Erastus Snow. Hence the name Snowflake.

In the 1880s, serious overgrazing in Texas resulted in catastrophic cattle losses and range deterioration. This is what drove ranchers like Beau Harcourt into the previously unexploited grasslands of the Little Colorado River Basin.

Unfortunately, by the turn of the century, the Texas experience had been repeated in Arizona.

Today, despite modern range management, the entire basin is seriously overgrazed.

Center Point Large Print
600 Brooks Road / PO Box 1
Thorndike ME 04986-0001 USA

(207) 568-3717

US & Canada:
1 800 929-9108
www.centerpointlargeprint.com